INK VINE

ELIZABETH BROADBENT

Undertaker Books
www.undertakerbooks.com

UNDERTAKER BOOKS
www.undertakerbooks.com

PRAISE FOR INK VINE

"Elizabeth Broadbent combines a steamy love story with important observations about desperation, fear, and acceptance. *Ink Vine*, with its elements of dark fantasy and botanical horror, reminded me of *True Blood*!"

—Christi Nogle, author of the Bram Stoker Award winning first novel *Beulah*

"A stunning debut with a narrative voice so strong, you'll feel the swamp breathing down your neck. Eerie and very moving."

—Tim McGregor, author of *Eynhallow* and *Wasps in the Ice Cream*

"*Ink Vine* is a lush and deliciously queer Southern Gothic romance about desire and the things we will do to sate it. Broadbent's richly drawn characters and smart, evocative prose gives new meaning to the phrase 'blossoming love.' Emerald's longing—for acceptance, for love, for something more—haunts every word and sets the stage for a beautiful narrative about acceptance, self-discovery, and the power of connection."

—Jolie Toomajan, editor of *Aseptic and Faintly Sadistic*

Surprise, Bear.

I love you.

INK VINE

In the wan gas station light, I counted my night's haul. Mint-new, the two hundred in twenties felt crisp, with the clean scent of untouched money. The ones and fives varied from ATM-stiff to flannel-soft. I liked to think about those old bills, where they'd been and who might've used them. I imagined little kids ordering soda, noses poking above convenience-store counters, or old men shuffling through a pharmacy line. I tried to ignore the reality of back pockets and sweaty palms. Customers sucked.

Two hundred and eighty—a middle kind of take-home, good for a Wednesday. I stuffed all but ten into my purse. Bugs hummed as I strode through the hot-breathed summer night. Damn global warming. Rich people and their private jets would kill us all, sweat us to death in the meantime. After a sweltering night at the club and a twenty-minute drive without air conditioning, my hair stuck to my neck. I'd have chopped it to my shoulders if I could, but my best friend, Alyssa McAllister, she swore guys liked long hair. "Then they can think about pulling it," she'd say, and I'd make a face. She didn't have to say it made me look younger, not that I didn't look seventeen already, and guys liked that even better. Barely legal dancers made the most money. It's ick, but life is ick all over. You'd think you'd get used to it, but you never do.

The Gas N Go's cowbell clanged in the four-thirty a.m. quiet, and Zeke glanced up from his porno mag. "Lookit you, Emmy Joiner," he said. I tried not to wince at my name in his mouth as he flicked greasy hair from his forehead. "You take a few minutes, you can earn some extra cash."

I didn't want to blush. The ugly light washed my skin white, and he'd see. "Pack of Parliament Lights, please."

"What's with you?" He made no move toward the cigarettes. "You'll fuck strangers, let alone those asshole McAllister boys, but you got none for me? I known you your whole life."

"I asked for a pack of Parliaments," I said. We stepped through the same crap every night I stopped in, but Lower Congaree shut down at eight. Unless I wanted to wait til eleven a.m., when Party Town #3 opened, I was SOL.

"I asked you to step out back with me." Zeke's face twisted into a leer. "Or we can take a minute in the bathroom. I ain't particular."

I gathered up my last shreds of courage. "I'm a dancer, not a whore, and I got cousins bigger and meaner than you. Pack of Parliament Lights, please." I kept my hands below the counter so he didn't see them shake. Six months ago, the daycare center downtown closed, and I started working at that club. In a week, the whole town knew, and Zeke had been hassling me ever since.

He flipped the cigarettes onto the counter. When I passed him cash, he held it to his nose and smirked.

"Those bills were nowhere near anything fun, you sick bastard." Eyes down, I snagged my cigarettes and fled. Fuck the change. Zeke would only keep harassing me, and it wasn't worth the time or two-fifty.

My old Nissan sputtered, then caught. It would die soon, and twice I'd blown my get-out-of-town money fixing it. Where would I find enough cash for a new car? I wouldn't, and no one would drive me to the club—Mama and Aunt Tabby would make me work at the chicken plant. I lit a cigarette and tried not to think about it. Everyone tells you not to smoke, but there's not much good in the world, and you gotta snatch happy where you can. Rich people think they know best. They don't know anything. Try being poor. See how much your feet hurt. Poor people sweat to death 'cause they can't afford to fix their air conditioners, and they come home from work stinking like chicken poo. You'd smoke too, if only to kill the smell.

I pulled outta the parking lot. The swamp sang on every side, all insect chitter and tree frog screech. Lower Conagree's only traffic light blinked red. Downtown was deader than dead, quiet as a tomb and just as creepy. Empty storefronts stood out like missing teeth. When I was in high school, we'd walk from the Gas N Go to Party Town #3, then pay whatever homeless guy hung outside to buy us liquor. He'd always do it 'cause we were cute, and me and Alyssa would cart it to the Lot and get plowed. She was so pretty, all long, pale legs and blonde hair. She smelled like roses, too. Sometimes we'd sit too close, cramming into a pickup truck or someone's backseat, and I'd try not to think about it.

I couldn't tell Zeke what I really thought: *I like girls better, and even if I wanted a guy, it wouldn't be a miserable counter-jockey like you.* He'd only say something like, *I know what can cure you of that*, and that gas station was real empty at four a.m. Not that I'd ever been with a girl. Bi women in Lower Congaree knew enough to keep quiet.

Zeke didn't know the truth, but he harassed me anyway. I was a broke-ass Joiner. White-trash welfare queens, that's what everyone called us, and so what if most of my family needed SNAP to get by? Born poor, stay poor. There aren't any bootstraps to pull up or ladders to climb, not if you're a Joiner kid. We lived in trailers and worked under the table or at the chicken plant, always had. I could threaten Zeke with my cousins, but they were too sorry and too stoned to care about shit-talking. He knew it, too.

I left town's sad emptiness and pulled onto the swamp road. At least guys liked me. They panted after my blue eyes and long legs, and they figured a Joiner girl would do anything for a few bucks. I raked in more money when they tried for it, but I hated cashing in on my own poverty. *Even if you're not a whore, you gotta act like one,* Alyssa always told me. *If they think they have a chance, they'll keep handing you bills.* The wind snatched my hair and whipped it into tangles. One more time, I wished I could cut it off.

Aunt Tabby's trailer clung to a weedy patch of ground on the edge of the swamp, and three broke-down old cars hunched in its drive like guilty dogs. I parked in the yard and shuffled through the grass, careful for snakes. Mama couldn't make rent alone. She and Aunt Tabby got up at dawn to work at the Bessinger Poultry Plant, where they plucked chickens and tried not to get their fingers stuck in machines. My fifteen-year-old brother Jett went to summer school at nine, or not, depending on his mood. I loved him more than all the rest of them put together. 'Cause of me, he had new clothes, nice shoes, and money for lunch; damn if the other kids would laugh at him like they'd laughed at me.

You don't have to do that, Emmy, he'd say.

Hush up and take it, I'd tell him.

He didn't want them to laugh either, so he'd nod and take lunch money, or the earbuds, the new shoes I'd picked up on a special trip to Columbiana Mall, thirty miles and a world away.

My sister Diamond slept in. Six months pregnant, she was miserable with morning sickness, afternoon sickness, evening sickness—if I ever needed a reason to swear off guys, she gave me a damn good one. Diamond had worked in the chicken plant til she barfed all over a plucked hen. That's how she knew she was pregnant. Ever since, money was tighter. With one person unemployed, I could hardly save enough for gas and cigarettes. But there was no way around it. You did what you could with what you had.

My cousin Jackson lived with us til Aunt Tabby kicked him out. She said he'd end up dead or in prison, and we didn't need a drug bust in our lives. Jackson bought weed from Talitha Merle's swamp garden and sold it at a fifty-percent markup, still cheaper than that shit coming down from DC. Mostly better, too, and real green instead of vape pens. He could calculate fractions and cost quicker than a math teacher. Aunt Tabby still called him a deadbeat. But Jackson made bank, and my aunt could fuck right off to sunny California. Why should he slave away at the chicken plant when he pulled down more from dealing? He only sold pot, and only to people over eighteen, part of his deal with Talitha. She scared the hell outta me. People went to her for help instead of a doctor, and they said she was a witch. She visited Mama sometimes. Once I got brave enough to ask why she grew.

"'Cause it keeps a kid from working a shit job," she told me, whip-quick and just as sure.

"Ain't no one in town gonna bust Talitha," Mama said. "She's respectable."

Talitha smacked her shoulder. "Don't you badmouth me, girl. I'm no kind of respectable."

Talitha was definitely a witch. Pretty too—she had real hips, a D-cup, and long, dark hair. Too old for me, but pretty anyway. When she started up with her husband, Mama and Aunt Tabby laughed. "Aren't those girls crying now?" Aunt Tabby said.

"What?" I asked, glancing up from my homework. I was a senior in high school then and determined to graduate, no matter how much work it took.

"Talitha used to run 'round with girls sometimes," Aunt Tabby told me. "Wonder if that hot guy of hers knows she saw Lacey Gray 'fore she got married, and Miss High-and-Mighty Charlotte Lanier back when she was plain old Charlotte Price."

Mama turned from the stove, where she was adding frozen peppers to ramen. "Talitha never been serious 'bout anyone but that man she's got. She only saw girls on the side, and you know she only did 'cause she didn't want to deal with men."

Maybe she was never serious about those *girls*, I wanted to say. *Maybe she knew Lacey and Charlotte weren't right for her, or maybe she only wanted something casual.* Instead, I kept quiet. They asked me about guys sometimes. I lied.

I passed out cold after another long night. In the morning, I could shower the club's grossness off. Diamond slept like shit, one reason to wrap it up, and running water might wake her. She'd slam outta bed and stomp into the broken-locked bathroom, all dirty laundry and pink-mold tile.

If you got a respectable job, you wouldn't have to shower in the middle of the goddamn night, she'd shout, and the whole house would wake up to watch us argue.

I'd say, *You showered after every day of your respectable chicken-plant job, back before you got knocked up.*

Then Diamond would call me a tattooed whore. My mama, aunt, and brother would stand in the hall, silent. *Stop*, Jett would mouth, and I'd ignore him, feeling awful that he had to see it. I might have to storm out, 'cause you can't hit a pregnant girl, even if she is your sister. I'd have to call Alyssa and pray she'd pick up, then beg for a spot on her couch. Maybe one day, I could afford my own place. I saved everything I could, crossed my fingers, and hoped. It was hard. Mama didn't make me give her money, but she might as well have. Sighing loudly, she'd say, "How are we gonna afford groceries this week?" She wouldn't ask, not outright, but she'd give me a look, one loud as if she'd spoken. *I know you got money in your purse, Emmy Ann*, she'd be hinting, saying it without saying it at all.

So I'd hand her money. Mama kept a roof over our heads. What else could I do?

And I needed things. Not big ones, but little ones, and you'll die from a hundred cuts as sure as one big wound. I had to buy hair stuff, and snacks; I paid for my phone. I needed gas, and cigarettes, and I saved for my car insurance. Once in a while, I'd buy something I didn't need at all, something special, like a sparkly phone case or a box of fried chicken. Sometimes, you just break. Tired of saying no, no, no all the time, you need something in your life to say yes. Everyone snarks, "Well, you wouldn't be poor if..." and they'll tell you what you're doing wrong. Those people, they've never stood on the outside looking in. The whole world's a toy store, and you're the kid outside pressing your nose on the window.

I had to help Jett, too. Where was he 'sposed to get money for football fees, or phone minutes, or those dates he was starting to go on? Mama wouldn't give it to him. She'd say, *We can't afford that,* and one more time, he'd get left out, left behind. Kids are like any other herd animal; they'll tear at the weakest just to watch them bleed. When you're different, poor or shy or crooked-toothed, they'll go at you like a pack of feral hogs. You can't stop them—you can only offer up another victim. Pick at smaller, weaker kids, and the others will turn on them instead. It's survival, mostly. Playgrounds are a pretty feral place when you come right down to it. Jett needed all the help he could get.

So my move-out fund hardly existed. I tried my best. But poverty has a way of sucking you back. It's a whirlpool, always dragging you down, and you swim and swim just to keep your head above water. Only the strongest break out.

I was determined to be one of them.

AT NOON, I WOKE to a mostly empty house, Diamond snoring across the room. At least I had enough hot water. At least I had decent conditioner, deodorant, and a straightening iron. Thank God for small mercies. When you're as poor as the average Joiner, you learn to appreciate them.

Our kitchen window was small, and day craned to reach it. When I was little, I wished for a sunny morning kitchen, all honey-gold light. Afternoon drew breakfast's wreckage in dull grays. Dishes piled the stained countertop, and the faucet dripped like a cold nose. I shoved some utility bills aside and poured myself off-brand Rice Krispies. Diamond was still asleep, so I jammed my feet into a pair of old sneakers and slipped off down the swamp trail. If Mama and Aunt Tabby harassed me for dancing, they downright bitched about my walks. *You stay away from that swamp*, they'd say. *People walk in and don't walk out. You know so-and-so...* and they'd drone about that Carson kid vanishing or Ellis Rockland gone missing. Sometimes they'd get creative and rant about will o' the wisps that led to alligator-filled streams, or crows that spoke in human voices. All ridiculous. Everyone knew Beau Carson's brother killed him, and Ellis Rockland disappeared almost two decades before. The rest of it was superstitious bullshit.

I'd been escaping to the swamp since we moved in about five years before. Every time I walked under that green-leaf canopy, I waited, almost hoped, that something weird would happen. It never did. The swamp's green faded to gray in the long distance, and Spanish moss tangled like a sleeping woman's hair. The swamp seemed to have—I'd struggled to find the right word—a presence all its own. Something watched and waited there. Why did it scare everyone? The world would hurt you. The woods went about their own business. In the swamp, I didn't have to pretend I enjoyed giving those lap dances, not like at the club, where I smiled like a kid on school picture day, all the time thinking, *I like women, you worthless bastard, and even if I did guys, I wouldn't touch you.* Instead, I walked for miles. I could shed Emmy the stripper and become Emerald, jewel-bright and finally alive.

About forty minutes into the swamp, I found my favorite place, where a pretty stream curved around an enormous cypress. I settled into a mossy spot tucked between its knees. The world smelled like honeysuckle and growing things. No one would call me a useless Joiner there. No one would offer me money for sex. Zeke's words still stung: *You'll fuck them McAllister boys but not me?* So what if I'd lost it with Alyssa's cousin Whit, back when I was fifteen? But the sheriff caught us at the Lot in the back of Whit's pickup, and he raised holy hell. Whit got threatened with statutory, not 'cause I didn't consent—the whole town knew we'd been going out for six months—but 'cause that sheriff knew he could do it. If I was a rich-ass Lanier girl and Whit was a Nesmith boy, Nash Briggs would've driven on by. The less you got, the more they come after you. Ask me how I know.

Not that I particularly loved Whit or something. It seemed like time to lose it, so I did. I'd have rather been with a girl, but they were untouchable as the moon. Guys were easier, even if they smelled musky and waved their dicks around like little boys with play swords. A girl would've been better. A girl would smell pretty, like fancy mall soap, and we could've shared clothes and makeup, laughing in that sleepy quiet before breakfast. Another girl would never have called me a slut 'cause I danced. *You do what you have to,* she'd say, 'cause she understood—maybe she'd have to do it too, like Alyssa. *We know what you really like.*

"What are you doing out here all alone?" someone said into the swamp's deep quiet, and I startled so hard I almost fell in the creek. A girl with green eyes stood on the trail, a beautiful girl, all long legs and long, black hair—I liked long hair too, but I didn't think about pulling it. Tattooed vines climbed from her coppery ankles to her thighs, from her wrists to her shoulders. Their stems tangled and forked; I didn't recognize the plant, but her artist was very, very good.

"I asked what you were doing out here all alone," the girl said. She was smiling.

"I'm just—I go for walks," I replied, hating myself, 'cause of course I sounded stupid. I wasn't used to talking to beautiful girls, or beautiful anyone, really. Lower Congaree was a little short on beauty, and maybe that was the real reason I hiked into the swamp.

"I'm Zara. Zara Fenwick." She plopped down next to me like she'd been invited. Close enough that we were already friends, maybe. I'd never met anyone in that deep, cool forest, much less a pretty girl. "Who're you?"

I hesitated. Everywhere else I was Emmy the wild child, Emmy the stripper, Emmy the useless white trash. I inhaled that rich, ripe scent of fertile dirt. That smell meant safety. "I'm Emerald," I told her, and sat up straight, shoulders back, like Mama taught. Not that I wanted to think about Mama. I didn't want to think about any of them.

"You sure about that, Emerald?" Her shiny hair and perfect teeth seemed a world away from Lower Congaree. A brown dress rucked high on her thighs.

All around us, the swamp sang insect drone and birdsong, treefrog hymns and woodpecker taps. "Yeah," I said. "I'm sure. What're you doing here?"

"I asked you first, and you obviously walked in here so you didn't give me a good answer." She kept smiling. My heart thumped, partly from the scare and partly 'cause she was gorgeous.

"I was hiking. There's a path behind my house." I didn't say "trailer" and I didn't add "I share it with my mom and aunt," 'cause Zara had tattooed vines twining her calves and eyes like summer sunshine. She looked my age, but I didn't dare hope.

"I live around here." Zara flicked her hand like the queen of some familiar country. On the edge of town, then, like me. People like the Joiners, we didn't live in the middle of anything. We were the kind of people who clung to the world's weedy margins. "I never see anyone out here," she said. "Tell me everything about you, Emerald."

She must've been as lonely as me. Small towns are a special kind of lonesome. You know everyone and everyone knows you, but they stick you in a box and say, "This is so-and-so, and she's like this." Then they never change their mind. If you do something horrible, like kill a person or hurt a kid, then they say, "Well, I always thought she was like that. I could see it in her," like they have to be right, even in hindsight. Like they have to know you, even if they didn't, all along. I wondered if Zara saw that same sadness in me, right away, without even asking.

She was waiting. Zara sat with her elbow on her thigh and her chin in her hand, the perfect thinker, like that statue. Far away, crows called.

I might as well begin at the beginning. "I was born here in Lower Congaree—"

"No, no, no." Zara emphasized each word. "Lower Congaree is out there. This is the Congaree Swamp. Anyway. Keep going."

"So I was born in Lower Congaree?" I said it like a question, like I wasn't sure. I wanted to get everything right. "I've lived there all my life—I mean, we moved around a lot, but we stayed in town? I graduated from Congaree High School—"

"Oh, poor you." Zara swooped me into a sudden hug. Her dark hair smelled like honeysuckle and broken leaves. "That's so awful. They're terrible there, aren't they? And you couldn't tell anyone you liked girls because they'd hurt you."

I leapt up. "I'm sorry, I have to go." No one knew my secret. The swamp was safe. How could she tell?

"You don't have to go." Zara tugged me down again. "Stop freaking out and keep telling me about you. It's different here. What do you do all day?"

The sun stretched long, pale fingers through the trees, and wind whispered in the branches. If I listened hard enough, it would tell me stories I was never meant to know. The swamp *was* different. There, no one called me names or offered me money to fuck. Mama didn't shout about my job. I wasn't Emmy Joiner, shoved into a neat little box and scared of the whole wide world. "I don't know," I said. "I sleep late and—read, watch TV, mess around on my phone, I guess. I, uh, work at night." I had to say it and what would Zara think? "I dance. I mean, at work. That's what I do. You know, exotic dancing."

"Oooh." Maybe Zara was looking at me. Staring at the trees, I couldn't stand to peek. "I bet guys like that. I bet you're good at it, too. You're so pretty."

I almost sagged onto the moss with relief. "Uh, thanks. I was scared—I worried you'd think—I don't know. You know what people think about dancers."

"It's so stupid." Zara's laugh fit with the birdsong and rustling leaves. "If you're pretty, why shouldn't people look? I want to see you dance sometime. Tell me more, Emerald."

When she used my real name again, something hurt inside me uncurled. Zara knew I was a bisexual stripper, and she called me Emerald. She hadn't run away. So I told her about living with my mama and aunt, and about Diamond bitching, and Jett skipping school. "They call us trailer trash," I said. "Guys always think I'm a prostitute 'cause I'm a broke-ass Joiner, and what wouldn't we do for money?" I wanted to slump against that cypress tree and close my eyes. Just thinking about it, that loneliness flooded me again, like no one knew me and no one ever would. "They're awful. We can't catch a break, you know? And if they knew I was bi they'd lose it. It's bad enough that I dance. If they knew I liked girls—"

"They're horrible." When I dared to glance at Zara, she was watching me. "I hate them, too."

"I could've gone to college." My throat went tight, like I'd swallowed a marble. "I mean, maybe. If I tried harder. Mama said college was a waste of time and money, so I didn't bother." She also said college was for rich kids and we were poor as dirt. I didn't want to tell Zara that. I didn't want to say that girls like me didn't go to college, even if we dreamed of it, 'cause we didn't fit in. Looking down their noses at me, those pretty rich girls would say things like, *Where are you from again?* and *What did you say your parents do?* Decent people have married parents, or at least divorced ones. Having kids without a man attached is trashy, and respectable daddies don't skip town.

"They're wrong about you. You deserve better than they treat you, Emerald." Zara picked up my wrist. When she traced the flower there, I went very still. She tucked her chin like a Disney deer. "I like your rose," she told me. "Do you have any more?"

My palmetto and crescent moon had taken six sessions, and I couldn't miss the chance to show it off, especially to another girl with ink. I'd saved for a year to get that tattoo. All my anger and sadness seemed to lift up and float away. I turned and pulled my tank a little lower. "It goes all the way down my back," I said.

"Let me see."

Was she flirting? Was this how one girl told another, *I like girls too, and I like you in particular?* But I took my clothes off every night, so I yanked my shirt up to my neck.

Soft fingers trailed over my spine, and I shivered like someone had dripped cold water on my back. People touched me all the time, but not like that. They groped and pawed, even Whit—maybe especially Whit, and Mel Heyward, and all those other guys. I wasn't a whore like they said, but I didn't stay Mother-Mary-pure, either.

"This is really beautiful," Zara told me.

"I like yours, too," I said.

"Thanks." She stretched out her arm, like she was examining them herself. "I like them a lot. They turned out well, don't you think?"

The next step baffled me. Did it always go so quick? I didn't know the dance steps.

"You're so pretty," she told me. "I haven't seen such a pretty girl in a long time." *Me either*, I could've said, but I didn't. I couldn't talk. My skin goosebumped under her touch. "I think I want to kiss you."

"Excuse me?" Wind murmured high in the tupelo trees; the insect whir and birdsong sunk to a strange quiet. "Uh, we're moving really fast—"

"That doesn't matter. I feel like I know you already. Do you want to kiss?" Zara's fingers drifted over me, all the better for their tickly-light dawdling. A gorgeous girl was stroking my back, and it couldn't be that different from kissing a guy, not really. I'd done plenty of that. So I shimmied my shirt down and faced her. If she wanted it so bad she could make the first move, I told myself. Really, I was too scared to do it myself.

"So pretty," Zara said. She rose to her knees and kissed me. Her lips were softer than any guy's, soft as the snowflakes I'd never seen, not in real life. Zara pulled me close and her pretty breasts pressed mine. I dared to slip my tongue past those pouty lips. I'd have done anything for lips like hers.

When her gentle fingers found my nipple, my breath caught. She played with it, then pulled back and pinched. Desire tap-danced low in my belly. "D'you like that?" she asked, like she couldn't tell. "You're fun."

Couldn't I touch her if she touched me first? I cupped her breast. She didn't stop me so I thumbed her nipple, and it tightened to a wicked eyeful under her thin dress.

"Like that," Zara said. When she kissed me again, her teeth nipped my lip. I'd wanted a girl's warm curves for so long, and this pretty stranger seemed unbelievable, like a spell or an answered prayer. She drew me nearer and her finger slipped between my cheeks. No one had ever touched me there, not ever, and its gleaming newness caught my breath.

Then she stopped.

I made my eyes wide and begging, a kid asking for one more piece of candy.

"Nope." Zara tapped my nose like you'd bop a disobedient puppy. "That's enough. You can meet me here again tomorrow. Same time."

"But—"

She popped to her feet. "Tomorrow. See you tomorrow."

I couldn't let her run away so fast. Had I done something wrong? I must not have, 'cause she wanted to see me again, but I couldn't help thinking it anyway. "We just started—"

Zara was already striding down the trail.

Want simmered as I tramped home. I slipped against myself and that want soared into need. My black undies soaked through. Mama and Aunt Tabby were at work. Maybe—but when I slid in my bedroom door, face flushed, Diamond was still snoring. Goddammit. I couldn't even get myself off in peace. My whole body hummed and there was nothing to do about it. After I pulled off my cutoffs, I flopped into bed. Diamond had to fuck around and get knocked up. I had to be poor enough to share a room. I closed my eyes and wished for somewhere else. But mostly, I wished for Zara.

I woke up sometime around four. Work started at seven, so I spent an hour straightening my hair and doing my makeup, then wandered to the kitchen for dinner. I always got dressed at the club, even if the backstage room skeeved me out, 'cause Mama raised holy hell if she saw my clothes.

You look like that Britney Spears video, she'd say, flipping at my plaid skirt. I wouldn't know what she meant, but I'd keep my face blank and my mouth shut. A long time ago, I learned to treat her harassment like a person might treat a hurricane: You can't stop it; you can only nail up the shutters and pray. Mama was real big on respect. You didn't talk back, and you sure as hell didn't tell her no. You just took whatever she doled out, nodded your head and waited for it to end. *Always walking outta here looking like a whore. It's one thing to be one and another to look like it. D'you know what people think of our family 'cause of you?* On and on. It'd only make me angry, bottled-up anger that eventually would explode and hurt everyone in its way. I'd dress later.

Jett was scribbling at summer school homework on the kitchen table. He'd flunk sophomore year if he didn't pass, and Mama would belt the hell outta him. *Why can't none of you kids work hard?* she'd shout. He might've been too old to cry, but he'd cry anyway. "Hey, Emmy," he said.

"Hey, Emmy baby," Mama called from the stove. Her back bent, and her shoulders slouched. Gray hair rooted behind her fake red. It made her look much older than forty-two. After a long day of work, she didn't have enough energy to dye her hair. I didn't blame her. "Jett, you get on that homework."

"Yes, ma'am," he muttered, and dropped his head again.

"Whatcha making?" I asked as I slid into a chair.

She hadn't turned around yet, but she would. Then the shouting might start. "Ramen with vegetables again."

We ate a lot of ramen. Mama dropped frozen veggies in it, but they couldn't disguise that miserable fake-chicken taste. You want to taste poverty, eat a pack of ramen or some Kraft mac and cheese—not Velveeta. You need bling to afford pre-made cheese sauce.

"How was work?" I asked. Me and Mama didn't have much to talk about; I had my life and she had hers. No one called her a whore, but she plucked feathers off dead chickens. You make compromises in the world, trade one flavor of bad for another. I've seen it too many times.

"Work was work," Mama said, which meant no better or worse than any other day.

Tummy first, Diamond waddled in. She was fit to bust but somehow hanging on. She'd wanted an abortion, but they killed Roe versus Wade and you couldn't get an appointment. Out-of-staters were crowding South Carolina abortion clinics. They'd probably outlaw it for good soon——one more reason to steer clear of guys.

"How was the swamp, Emmy?" my sister asked, 'cause she liked to start shit.

Mama whirled from the stove. "How many times have I told you not to go out there, goddammit!" she snapped. Jett winced and ducked lower, like he could escape as long as he hunched up small. "D'you know how many people disappeared back there? You might dress like a hooker at work, but we don't want nothing to happen to you!"

Of course she dragged my clothes into it. I sagged into a chair and waited for the storm tide to break. I was stupid, irresponsible, and didn't have the brains God gave a goose. I was about as sharp as a marble, and it was gonna be the death of me. Our kitchen was small, cramped with our table crammed in, and Mama's anger sucked up any room we had left. I focused on the scarred wall. There was the patched hole repaired before we moved in; its height and placement said someone punched it in. There was the grease stain from Aunt Tabby throwing spaghetti at Jackson, and a ghost of green body paint, made when Diamond's Halloween costume brushed a corner. Odd black marks curled like runaway punctuation. Someone should've stopped to scrub them, but no one had time or inclination.

Of course, smack in the middle of the shouting, Talitha Merle walked in. Maybe she'd knocked. Mama was yelling too loud to hear.

"What's this about?" Talitha asked. All that dark hair spilled down her shoulders, and I wished one more time that she wasn't so old or so married, and maybe didn't scare me half to death.

"Emmy wandered into the swamp again today!" Mama said. "We told her over and over, and she still walks on back there like she owns the thing. You talk some sense into her, Talitha. Don't nobody know that place like you."

Talitha sat across from me. She smelled like lavender and I tried not to think about it. "There's things in that swamp you never wanna see," she said, and her voice was low and serious, a teacher telling me I'd best buckle down and work or else. "Don't you go back there. You might not come out again, and you don't wanna know how I know that."

"Maybe I do," I said, 'cause I didn't have anything to lose. I'd already lost most things worth having, or I never had them in the first place. Our kitchen went very still then, the quiet that comes before a thunderstorm. Aunt Tabby had snuck in—the whole family was watching me get yelled at. We only had basic cable, and I guess it was better than TV.

"My own daddy disappeared into that swamp," Talitha told me. "He never came out again." Her steady, solemn voice told me she wasn't lying, either. I knew truth when I heard it.

"That what happened to him?" Mama asked.

"You don't go in that swamp," Talitha said, Mama's words passing like a breeze. "You hear me, Emmy? You'll regret it. You disappear, the sheriff won't go look more than two hundred yards into that muck. I know Nash Briggs, and he's smart enough to be scared."

I watched my hands. They were small and pale, my fingernails black as a goth girl's. "What if there are people back there?" I asked.

"There's nobody you wanna meet." Talitha still spoke in that serious, come-to-Jesus, get-your-life-straight voice. "People go in there, they come back changed. Like I said, nobody knows that more than me." She stood up, and a heaviness lifted. Just like that, the conversation was over. "I didn't mean to come during dinnertime," she told Mama. "I'll leave y'all be."

"No, no, sit down," Mama said, like I knew she would. We didn't have much but Mama never let anyone walk away from our table. So Talitha sat, and they ran through the usual Lower Congaree gossip—who got married, who got pregnant, who got thrown in jail. After about ten minutes, I said, "Well, gotta get to work, y'all," even though I didn't have to be there for another hour, and I'd miss dinner besides. Whatever. I could grab some fries at the club.

"Bye," Jett said, still hunched up. Mama scared the hell outta him.

"You remember what I said, Emmy Joiner," Talitha told me.

"Yes, ma'am," I replied, and I sort of meant it and sort of didn't. Luckily my car started again, and I fought with myself as I drove those dinky backroads, then the broad swamp highway. Everyone in town agreed that if Talitha Merle gave you advice, she was as serious as a heart attack and twice as urgent. But Zara had kissed me. She'd called me Emerald, and her skin was soft as satin. I didn't want to give her up on Talitha Merle's say-so.

Drainage ditches lined both sides of the road; people said sleek-fat catfish swam in them. They said those fish would gobble you down to bare bones. I wasn't sure if I believed it, but I sure as hell didn't care to learn the truth. Talitha and Mama were sorta right. You didn't fuck with the swamp. People in Lower Congaree recited that like one of God's own commandments, and if I hadn't been going back there for so many years, I'd have been scared, too. But I never saw anything strange in the swamp, not once, not even a will o' the wisp. I had to decide who to listen to, those tired women or my own yearning need. I couldn't make up my mind. Sometimes you just pick your poison and pray.

Sunset was still an hour off when I pulled into the Bottoms Up parking lot. I hated coming to work in the daylight. It felt grimy and strange, like fingernail dirt that won't wash out, no matter how hard you scrub. The club's outside looked dingy, sad, all black walls and cigarette butts mashed in the dirt. Some greaseball guys were hanging near the front door. Not smoking, not talking, just standing there like they had nothing better to do. I walked past with my eyes down, but I felt them staring.

Like usual, Noah was behind the bar. His daddy owned the place, and he was more proud of that than he should've been, but I liked him anyway. Between his puppy-dog eyes and messy hair, I tended to forget how big he was. Like a lot of guys in Lower Congaree, Noah spent his spare time doing bench presses, mostly 'cause there wasn't shit else to do. "Hey, girl," he said. "How you doing tonight?"

"I'm doing," I replied. *I kissed a girl*, I could've said. *Or rather, she kissed me. It was everything I hoped for. But Mama says I can't go into the swamp again, so I can't see her, and that's as bad as the kiss was good.* "Y'all calling in an order soon?" I asked instead. Bottoms Up had to serve food to serve liquor, so they sent out to The Roadhouse, a mile up the road. Noah's daddy Kurt owned that, too.

"Pretty soon, probably," Noah told me. "You want something?"

"Just some fries," I said.

"You want a drink before you get changed?" he asked.

Some girls got drunk before work—Noah would give two drinks on the house, strong ones, and more at a discount. He said it made the girls better dancers, and it did, mostly 'cause they stopped caring what people thought. They also stopped noticing where people put their hands.

"I'm good," I told him, like I said every night, and slid through the crowd to the dressing room. Bentley was already shaking what God gave her, and we had about twenty guys scattered around, most drooling over her and eating chicken wings—Thursday was twenty wings for fifteen bucks. Noah said his daddy lost money on the wings but made it up in drinks.

"Hey, Luna," said Savannah, half outta her clothes already. Everyone in town knew I was Emmy Joiner, but I had to pick a stage name—we all had them—so I picked Luna 'cause it sounded kinda gothy, with the moon and all. I dressed gothy, too, wore black undies and black nail polish. I'd have worn halters and collars and chains too, if I had enough courage. Guys like goth girls. They think we're more likely to do freaky stuff, and any guy who tells you he doesn't want that is lying. They like you on your knees, and if they don't, it's 'cause they want to be on their knees instead. Dance for six months and you'll know it's true.

I thought about that, and about picking a new name and why I did it. I wanted to tell Zara. *I can't even be myself at that club*, I'd say, then I remembered that I might not see her again. Sadness dropped like a sick weight. I had to decide if I'd listen to Mama or go my own way, and

Mama could make me listen. She'd tear my life into misery with shouting arguments, and it was easier sometimes, quicker, to duck my head and say, "Yes, ma'am." People will tell you to follow your heart, but it can be like struggling to swim when you're tied to an anchor. Sometimes the battle isn't worth it. They'll drown you in the end.

I shoved it away. Best not to dwell on disappointment, and I had to smile, smile, smile. I'd be sad after work. Just then, I needed to hustle. *You're Luna*, I told myself as I stripped to my black thong. *You like guys, and they like you back.* Wiggling, I wrangled on my garter belt, stockings, bra top, and high heels. I knew Luna real well by then. She was quieter than the other dancers, a good listener, sort of brainless and giggly. Guys loved her.

The night wore on like any other. The club was a kind of church, one where men came to worship bodies instead of God. Not women—they didn't particularly like women, and most of them had women at home, anyway. They wanted to get away from their women. "She doesn't love me anymore," they'd say when they got drunk enough. "I stay around for the kids. If I leave, I'll never see 'em again." Those were the nice guys. Others would tell you that their woman let herself go, which generally meant she had a baby. "Well, who put that baby there?" I'd want to ask. Some guys would outright tell you their wife was a bitch. "She treats me like shit," they'd say, and you'd know there was another side to that story.

You'd think they came in 'cause they were horny. Most were, but horniness will only get you in the door. Those guys stuck around to play make-believe. Whether or not they whipped it out, they wanted to pretend they were Hugh Hefner. These were broke-ass men who worked all day at a chicken plant or lumber company or lawn care service, places that paid them minimum wage to shut up and take whatever their bosses handed them. They wore dirty jeans; they smelled like sweat and cigarette smoke. The type of guy who came into the club, he didn't have much to offer, or he didn't think he did. So he paid us to play king for a day, and we made him feel sexy, wanted. We gave him what real life promised and snatched back—call it control, or love, or a sense of self-worth. We traded in lost fantasies and fairy tales. Remember that next time you see a club. They call us sex workers, but we aren't, not really. We don't sell sex. We hand out dreams.

Caught on mirrored walls, our reflections went on and on, a miniature infinity; sometimes I liked to think about that and sometimes I didn't. Hard-edged but somehow vague, the club always seemed stuck in a hazy hour between midnight and one, and after a while, you felt the backbeat in your fingertips. Everything smelled like sex and cigarettes—it's illegal to smoke inside, but when the sheriff's deputies were sucking down Marlboro Reds, no one gave a fuck. Recirculated air dried your mouth, and people drank too much. Even me, sucking down plain Cokes, my glass rim would go sticky with lip gloss, and I'd remind myself not to chew ice.

We were black-lit and beautiful in it. When our DJ played the first scraping notes of "Closer," I stepped onstage. Every time, I did the same dance, hardly a dance at all. Bright stage lights drew the men as a dark, faceless crowd. I focused on that anonymous dark and moved the way they liked, all slinky grace. They slid money in my thong. I shook my ass. They wanted me, and I wished they were girls. After two songs, my back hurt and my feet ached. I was working the tables when, like every night, one of the guys called me Emmy.

"I'm Luna here, baby," I told him, all fake smiles while my stomach pitched. When I sat in his lap, he grabbed my side. I managed not to cringe.

Tuck, our bouncer, only stopped guys who pawed what he called our "bathing suit areas."

"How much d'you charge to go out back?" the guy whispered.

"I don't do that, honey." I laughed like he'd said something funny.

I almost recognized his weak eyes and dull hair; maybe he was one of those Wheeler guys. Reverend Jack Wheeler, who preached at the Holiness church, he had about a dozen dirty-faced kids. Trust the preacher's son to show up at a strip club. "I got a hundred bucks here that says you do more than dance," the guy told me.

"I'd cost a lot more than that." I smiled again. A strip club will teach you to smile at terrible things if you didn't already know how. Me, I learned real small. I learned to smile when Mama didn't have much money for Christmas, and when boys at school looked up my skirt; when Mama made ramen for the fourth night in a row and teachers glanced down my tank top. If your Thanksgiving turkey comes from the food pantry, the world teaches you to tolerate a lot.

"Two hundred," the guy said, and he raised his voice to make sure I heard.

I shook my head again, and that smile never moved. I could've been Miss America.

"I can do two fifty but no more," he told me.

I wanted to say, *If you ask me that one more time, I'll get the bouncer to kick your ass out, and he might take that phrase literally. I don't like guys, not ones like you.* Instead I giggled and focused on my toes. "You're really cute, but I can't. I'm a good girl." They liked to hear that, and his arm tightened around my waist. He wasn't cute at all.

The guy settled on a thirty-dollar lap dance. He'd really thought I'd fuck him for a little more than the price of three of them. Some of the girls might've done it, or at least held out for three hundred. Elecktra probably would've. She worked every night 'cause she wanted her kids to have Barbie Dream Houses and soccer gear. I hoped those kids loved her. I hoped they didn't know how their mama got money for a Nintendo Switch.

I shimmied through the low light and cigarette smoke. Elektra was doing her best by her babies, and it shouldn't've mattered what she did. *Nothing sadder than a C-section scar on a stripper*, a guy said once, and I balled my fist but kept smiling. He didn't know a goddamn thing, not one. I thought about that guy while I danced—the light drawing his face in sharp, mean angles, the smirk twisting his mouth. I pushed my tits in the Wheeler kid's face and thought about how you did the best you could with what you had. I made more money than Mama and Aunt Tabby. I made more money than Jackson. I was saving up for my own place, and every dancer says it but I was saving up for an education, too. Not college but some kinda school, cooking or massage or cosmetology. Anything that wouldn't see me breaking my back in a chicken plant. So I played with my tits, and I rubbed against that guy, and I hoped he kept his hands planted on the arms of that chair.

Finally, the dance ended. They always do. Someone said once that as long as you hold your breath, you can do anything for ten minutes. Maybe they were right. I took my cash and grabbed my fries from the bar. I could've carried them back to the dressing room, but it was ick, and my eyes would've got accustomed to the brighter light.

I ate. I used the dancer's bathroom. I fended off requests for a private room—guys liked to get the girls back there and ask for sex. When they played Marilyn Manson's "Tainted Love," I stepped onto that strange altar and took my clothes off again. I imagined the hooting men were pretty girls, and I smiled. I wished the men watching me were Zara. I'd probably never see her again. I tried not to think about that. I tried not to think about her sunshine eyes and her soft lips on mine. She'd kissed me like I was special, like we had time and time and time.

We closed around four on Thursday nights. Sometimes that felt like nine at night and sometimes it felt like noon—you lose track. I was giggling with an old guy when Noah yelled for last call, and that Wheeler kid slipped up behind me. "I can do three hundred," he said into my ear. I could've reeled away from his booze-breath.

I made myself laugh. "I told you, I'm a good girl."

The old guy paid his bar tab and handed me an extra twenty. Old guys are usually good that way. They're grateful for someone who makes them feel young again. It's a sad kind of magic, but the best girls can do it without trying. I kissed his cheek and ducked out to the dressing room before the customers left and the lights went up. The club's a special kind of sad in the light, all empty glasses and spilled drinks, like a daydream gone stale. I didn't want to see it. After I changed, I stood at the door and waited for Noah to take me to my car. He won't let dancers walk through a dark parking lot alone.

"Hey, three fifty." The Wheeler boy ducked out of the shadows as I leapt and clutched my chest.

"You scared me!" I scolded cutely.

"I'm serious, three fifty." He smelled like cheap cigarettes and cheaper beer. I almost retched. "You know you'll do it for that much."

And maybe it was tempting. I'd probably pulled three hundred that night, not bad for Thursday, but three hundred and fifty was almost a third of our rent. For the teeniest sliver of a moment, I saw Mama's gray part and creased forehead, a pen tapping her lips as she scribbled numbers on envelopes. But she'd've said, *Where'd all this money come from, Emmy Ann?* I'd never crossed that line, not once. I didn't want to make their rumors true. Even if I did, I'd have hated every second.

"I told you, I don't do that." I smiled again. I had to.

He reached for my wrist, and that half-breath felt like falling down a long, dark well.

"Leave her the fuck alone!" There was Noah, shoving him back. "Don't you fucking touch her, y'hear me? Get outta here before I call the sheriff and your dad in that order, you fucking Jesus freak."

He was definitely a Wheeler, then. His daddy might've kicked his ass all the way to Sunday morning if he got caught at the club. He wobbled for a second, spun, then almost fell. Then he spit at Noah's feet and staggered into the still, hot night.

"Sorry, Luna." Noah took my arm. "You shouldn't have to put up with that shit. It's 'cause you're pretty." He gave me one of those what-can-you-do-about-it smiles. "Lemme walk you to your car. We'll wait til he leaves, okay?"

I didn't get outta there til four-thirty, and Mama's alarm was blaring by the time I hit my bed. Diamond snored through it. On account of being so sick, she didn't have to work. She'd have slept with that Wheeler guy and kept the cash for herself. *Dress like a whore and you'll get treated like one,* Mama always told me.

I hated that she was right.

YOUR FIRST THOUGHT OF the day is important. My gramma always said that. She didn't mean the everyday "I have to pee," or "My alarm's going off." She meant that first deliberate thought, the one that cuts through your morning static. On Friday, I thought of Zara. *Tomorrow,* she'd told me. *I'll see you tomorrow.*

She wouldn't, I decided. Talitha had been telling the truth, and I ought not to walk back into that swamp, no matter how much I liked Zara. Goddammit. I'd finally met a girl, and I couldn't see her again. Maybe I'd run into her in town, at the Gas N Go or McAllister's grocery store. I could hope. Strange I'd never seen her before—Lower Congaree was so small. Maybe she'd just moved in, or maybe she kept to herself. Diamond was still snoring, so I slipped into the bathroom. When I finished my shower, I dressed and wandered into the kitchen.

It was a lazy summer morning, and the trees had gone the dark, tired green that comes in August's deepest dog days. It hadn't rained in two weeks. The grass was baked brown, and even the weeds had crisped. Our window units hummed endlessly, tunelessly, trying to keep up with the hundred-degree heat. I was settling breakfast when Diamond walked into the kitchen. She grabbed a banana, and we sat at the table together, two people in one house without much to say to each other.

"How d'you feel this morning?" I finally asked.

"Like shit," she replied around her banana. "I wish this baby would hurry up and come already."

She had three more months. She probably didn't want to think about it. I wouldn't, if I were her.

"You know, you oughta listen to Mama," she said.

"About what?" I asked. Mama harassed me about so many things, and Diamond could've meant any of them. Crispy Rice clumped my mouth. I'd hear it from her, whatever it was.

"About work. You can get a good job—"

My spoon splatted my milk. "I make good money, and it's not the chicken plant."

Her eyes went piggy and mean, and I knew we'd skip through the same argument then. The words changed, but its tune stayed the same. "What, you too good to work there? You think your shit don't stink? You don't take your clothes off to work in the chicken plant, and you don't fuck the chickens."

I sagged into my chair. "You gonna talk like that when your baby gets here?"

"Maybe not," she said. "Mama always talked like that in front of you, and look how you turned out."

I stared at my Crispy Rice, already going soggy. I wasn't gonna eat it. Aunt Tabby would've harassed me for wasting food, but everything tastes bad when you're miserable, no matter how hungry you are. "I wish, just for once, that I could have an actual conversation with someone in this house,"

I said, mostly to myself, 'cause my sister didn't care. "Every time I try and talk, it's all 'Your clothes are awful' or 'Your job is awful' or 'Don't do this or that.' No one cares how I feel about any of it."

"Yeah, 'cause you're wrong," Diamond said, mouth still full. "If someone hurts you at work, it'll be your fault." She grabbed another banana. I dumped my bowl into the sink. Normally I'd have drank the milk, but I couldn't stomach it. Diamond really believed that old lie. *Well, she asked for it*, people would say. The rest of my family probably agreed.

Pieces fell into place then, like I'd dumped a bucket of blocks and formed a perfect tower. My job and clothes made me fair game. If someone grabbed me or jumped me in the parking lot, they'd say, *Well, he wouldn't have done it if...* then rant about my clothes or my job. *Emmy Ann, you brought this on yourself*, Mama would tell me. Aunt Tabby and Diamond would nod along with her.

No one fought for me, not ever. The worst things could happen. I could get beaten, raped, murdered. I could disappear. They still wouldn't fight.

I balled my fist. I could've punched a hole in the wall then, jammed knuckles and broken bones on that cheap drywall. Crying, I'd have cradled that hand and slid to the floor. I'd have sobbed from the pain, and I'd have sobbed with the betrayal. They thought I deserved it. I couldn't decide which I wanted more, the smashing or the sobbing. If I stayed, I'd give in to one or the other, then Diamond would tattle to Mama and I'd get it twice. *Well your sister was right*, she'd say. It would've sucked the wind outta me, like a sucker punch you never saw coming. I had to get out. Zara would understand. Just then, I didn't care if the Lord Jesus Christ had come down from heaven and told me to stay away from that swamp. Someone understood. I only had to walk in and find her.

Diamond would blab to Mama. She'd always been a big mouth, that kid who ran to tell who hit who or piped up to say so-and-so's lying. Diamond could holler all the way to hell, 'cause I might've been a dancer but no one knocked me up. One lasts a hell of a lot longer than the other. Her baby daddy wasn't gonna help her, either—Brant Wilcox was just as poor as us, and pissed at her besides. He said that baby was her choice and her fault, like his dick had nothing to do with it. They hadn't spoken in two months. That baby would be born poor, and like every other Joiner, she'd die poor, too.

I fumed about all that as I stalked through the swamp. Diamond was one of those people who couldn't be unhappy on her own—she had to spread it around, like a bad cold. Her baby would come up in that. She'd either learn to dish it out or get quiet and take it.

Eventually I calmed down and started to notice the world again. A beamed ceiling of tree branches wove overhead, and every shade of green was different, each one new. Mud clotted the low places; birds sang like a Sunday choir. I wished I knew their names. Under the tall, green cypresses, the temperature dropped at least twenty degrees. Humidity clung like my mother never had, like the swamp's warm breath.

I could picture it then, the whole swamp spreading around me, all those trees and creeks and snarled green vines. If you looked, if you paid attention, you could see a whole world blooming. Birds sheltered in the trees; small creatures tucked themselves into the brush. Fish and frogs hid in deep-running creeks. Life seemed brand-new there, and maybe it was. Maybe we all came from the swamp, I thought. Maybe everything started in a place like this, where water met land and married in a glorious mud-puddle confusion.

When I rounded the corner to my favorite spot, Zara leapt from the moss. "You came!" she said, throwing her arms around me, and I realized I'd been so angry about Diamond I forgot to be nervous. Zara wore a short green dress, fraying on its edges. It was thin and I tried not to think about that. Instead, I concentrated on the smell of her hair, like honeysuckle in the rain.

"I worried you wouldn't come," she said, pulling me down to the moss. "Now, sit down and tell me everything."

"Before I do, where d'you live?" I asked. "My mama gets mad about me coming out in the swamp—"

Zara's laughter bubbled like a clear, bright stream. "There's nothing for you to be worried about back here."

"Mama and this friend of hers said it's dangerous." I phrased it carefully: *dangerous*. Under that tangly green canopy, among the golden flowers, I couldn't stand to accuse the forest. It held us in its kind, cupped hands. Trees murmured in the high-up wind, and the little creek babbled. It seemed to speak words I'd known once and forgotten. I could've curled up on that moss and slept.

Zara rearranged her long legs. Her tattooed vines were knotty, wild. I imagined tracing their stems right up her thighs. "Maybe it's dangerous if you think it's dangerous. Or maybe people just don't like it. Think about the word 'swamp.' It's so ugly. Why would you give this place such an ugly word?"

I'd never thought of that. It *was* an ugly word, short and squat, with a sound like spitting. "It seems terrible, doesn't it?" I said. "I've never seen anything strange back here, not once. But Mama said people disappear—"

"People can't *disappear*, Emerald." Zara petted the moss like it was a kitten, back and forth, back and forth. "Maybe they get lost, or go somewhere better, but they don't vanish into thin air."

"I guess not," I said. She was right. It sounded ridiculous.

"So tell me what you've been up to." She picked up my hand again, and her fingers tickled my wrist. "I want to hear everything."

So I told her about work, about that Wheeler boy, about Diamond and the terrible things she'd said. Zara's mouth puckered, and her brow drew down. The longer I spoke, the madder she looked. It felt good to see my anger written on someone else's face. "That's *horrible*," she said. "Like it's better to work at that awful plant. At least you aren't killing anything. I'm glad you came out here. You need to get away from all that."

"Thank you." I focused not on her face, but those vines circling her arms.

"They're awful," she told me. "Really, you shouldn't have to put up with them."

I wanted to run from that subject, run and never look back. The forest cradled us like its favorite secret. Maybe we were. I could've believed it. *It loves us*, I thought, then, *Don't be stupid. Forests can't love people.*

"Tell me about you," I said.

"I told you the other day. There isn't much to tell. I don't know. I like to watch birds and swim and hike." She flipped my wrist. "I really do like your rose, Emerald."

I wanted her to say my name over and over. "I love your tats, too." I was about to ask Zara if she liked movies when she raised my wrist to her lips and kissed its sensitive underside. Without meaning to, I shivered.

"I think I should kiss you again." Her eyes caught and held mine. She saw me and she didn't flinch, or make a face, or say, *Well Emmy, you know you shouldn't do that.* Instead, Zara seemed to wait. I managed a nod, and she leaned closer. "You're so pretty, Emerald," she told me, and her lips brushed mine when she spoke, like a butterfly kiss. I'd always wanted a kiss like that, one that said, *We can take our time.* When my arms went around her, our chests touched, and Zara's nipples were tight little buttons.

"Lay down. Here." Zara pulled me to the moss. It smelled earthy, like good, rich soil. Somehow, that made everything better—like the forest had built us a little hideaway. Brush bowed above us; leaves rustled, whole stories sung by the wind. Zara's legs tangled into mine.

Her palm rested against my cheek, and she kissed me like I was something beautiful, breakable. My fingers wove into her long hair. Zara's lips were more delicate than any guy's, and kinder. I tried to think about that, not her long thigh pressed between mine. Mine pressed her too, and I couldn't think about that soft heat either. As her hand trailed down my neck to my back, I dared to pet her side, a perfect in-and-out curve. I'd wanted it forever. Her hip was a revelation, her waist a dream. I couldn't help wiggling closer.

"I like this," she whispered, and her hand darted between us. When she cupped my breast, I sighed and arched my back. My shorts tightened, and their seam pressed my clit. As I rocked my hips, that sweet pressure slid over me. I was already getting wet.

Zara didn't rush. She drew my nipple into a peak, then thumbed it softly. When I brushed hers, it had tightened to a hard nub. I wanted to feel it between my lips, but I didn't know how to get there. Those feminine curves baffled me, like a puzzle whose pieces I couldn't decode. She must've known. "Like that," she said, words half a kiss. "You can do it harder."

When I pinched her nipple, she sighed and pressed against my leg. That warmth had become almost hot, and her pussy slipped against me. If her curves confused me, that part seemed unimaginable.

I wanted her so much, but other thoughts barged in. Zara hadn't told me much about herself—where she lived, how old she was. What if she just liked coming out here and hooking up? Maybe it wasn't me she liked. Maybe she liked anybody rather than somebody. When you're lonely, you'll latch onto anything. I couldn't stop wondering about that, and I pulled back.

"What?" Zara's arched brows drew together, an adorable confusion. "What's wrong?"

"Where d'you live?" I asked.

Her nose wrinkled. "I told you. Not far from here."

I forced myself to sit up. I wanted to keep kissing her, but fear rolled in my belly. If this wasn't something I wanted, better to figure that out right away. I had to say it. She might think I didn't like her, and only that gave me enough guts to speak. "I don't know much about you," I admitted.

"Oh, *Emerald*." Her laughter was like wind in the trees. "You're so worried about so many things that don't matter. I swear, I really like you. Is that so hard to believe?"

"What if it was?" I asked. "If you liked me, you'd tell me more about you."

"Okay." She shoved up. Her dress bunched on her thighs, and those vines did go all the way up, at least as far as I could tell. "I'm boring. I feed the birds. Did you know there are ivory-billed woodpeckers way, way deep in the forest? People don't believe it but it's true. They're back there. They aren't gone."

I didn't know much about those, but I heard they were extinct. "Really?"

"Yeah. That's why we have to protect places like this. People think they can take and take and take. They think they can burn oil and kill trees and it won't matter. There are otters in these creeks. They won't live in polluted water. If we don't stop..." And she was off. Zara told me about people throwing trash from their cars, and dumping tires in the woods, and carving their names on trees. "There were so many fireflies once," she said. "You wouldn't believe it, Emerald. They'd all light up at once, and whole fields would turn bright as day."

Mama said once that when she was a little girl, she scooped fireflies into jars, and they lit her room all night long. Lower Congaree is famous for its fireflies—we're one of the only places on earth where they blink at the same time, and tourists come from far away to see them. Strange how one person's everyday is someone else's miracle. Zara was almost in tears describing those pretty bugs. When she mentioned Carolina parakeets, how we'd torn up forests and starved those flocks of rainbow birds, her tears spilled over.

I picked up her hand. "It's awful," I said.

"It's horrible." She swiped at her nose. "And no one cares, Emerald. They don't care about it at all. I'm so angry. No one listens."

The cicadas had gone quiet. No birds sang, and no squirrels scuffled in the leaves. Only the stream burbled, on and on and on. The world seemed to hush, like that moment between a lightning flash and thunder. *Everything's listening*, I thought, then brushed it away.

"I'll listen," I told Zara. I would've given her anything when her big green eyes went wet, tears like dew on her lashes. I tried not to think of those parakeets. I'd never heard of them, and it seemed like one more symptom of a terminal sickness.

"We lost the parakeets a long time ago," she said, as if I'd spoken aloud. "A long, long time ago. I can still be mad. It won't bring them back, but I don't care." She gave me a sad little smile. "Now you know what I care about, I guess."

"It's beautiful even if it hurts," I said before I thought.

"What d'you mean?" she asked.

I winced. I'd sound even stupider than I already had. Sometimes I was good at that. I'd given up trying to talk a long time ago. I'd say something important, and no one listened, or they laughed, or they said, *Oh Emmy, that doesn't matter.* You learn silence that way. You shut up and take what the world hands out. It's a lonely kind of life, but at least no one's laughing at you. "I mean seeing how much you care," I tried to explain. "It's beautiful, but it's sad that you're sad, I guess. I don't know. It was dumb."

"No." She touched my cheek again. "You're exactly right. Tell me what you love that much."

I wished for a hoodie, at least something I could draw my fists into. I planted my hand on the moss instead and tried to concentrate on its pillowy softness. "I don't know."

"There must be something. No one cares about nothing."

I didn't want to say it. She wouldn't understand. "It's selfish and weird."

"I bet it's not." Zara slid her hand to my wrist again. "Tell me. I promise not to judge whatever it is."

I took a deep breath, like a running leap into deep water—the kind where you jump and hope you won't hit bottom. "I care about being myself."

"What do you mean?" Zara asked, and I could've watched those green eyes forever. They were the kind of eyes that would look, and keep looking, and see the very worst things without closing.

"I care about making myself into someone I wanna be, not who people say I am." Maybe that was the best way to phrase it. I was more than Emmy, or Luna, or that girl who danced for money. I wasn't a welfare mooch or a whore. I was Emerald. "I wanna save enough money to leave my mama's house," I said, real fast, like I had to get it out fast or I'd lose my nerve. "I wanna be around people who know me, I guess? I wanna be someone I can be proud of." I turned around and lifted my shirt. "That's why I got this." I gestured at my tattoo. "It's all South Carolina but it's more than that, too. The palmetto's the state tree 'cause of that Revolutionary War battle. We had to learn about it over and over in school—you probably did too. The one with the fort made out of palmettos. When the British shot cannonballs at it, they bounced off. I wanna be like that, you know? The type of person that no one can hurt. And I like the moon 'cause it changes, but it's always the same. It's feminine, I guess. I don't know."

It was too much and I drew my knees to my chin. I'd never told anyone why I picked my tattoo. It seemed like too much to say, like I'd pulled a secret from my chest and held it in my hands, a broken bird.

"That's a good tattoo." Zara trailed her fingers over it, like she was tracing it with her eyes shut. "Those are good things to want, Emerald. See? You do care about something. It's the most important thing to care about, too—yourself. If you could get another tat, what would you get?"

"No contest," I said right away. I'd already thought about it, but no way could I afford something so intricate—my palmetto had cost me more than I wanted to think about. "I'd get vines on my legs like yours."

"Would you?" She almost squealed. Far away, crows cawed. Leaves whispered riddles, and sunshine slid through the canopy. The whole world seemed happy.

"Yeah," I said. "I love the way the vines look, but it's more than that, too." I thought about how to say it. "I feel like I can be myself here. So I'd want those vines to remind me who I am. Which is kinda weird, 'cause you had them first, but I don't think it matters." I curled up a little more. "I could never afford them."

"You never know," Zara stood up. "Meet you tomorrow?"

My heart skidded, like it slipped inside my chest, and the world seemed sad again. "What? Already? But we were having fun."

"Gotta go, sorry, Emerald," Zara said, and one more time, I loved her saying my name.

"If you gimme your number, we can text," I said, then remembered that I'd stormed out without my phone. "If you have yours, I'll put mine in, and—"

"Don't have anything with me," she said. "And I'll never remember your number. I'm terrible at numbers. You can meet me again, right?" She caught her lip between her teeth. I wanted to kiss it again. "See you tomorrow, Emerald."

"Where d'you *live*?" I called, but she was already bouncing down the trail. "Do you have a name on Insta or something, where I can message? Zara?"

She was already gone. The swamp had come alive again, crows cawing, cicadas whirring, a woodpecker tap-tapping far away. It reminded me of the ivory-bill. As I walked back to the house, I thought about the ivory-bill, and I thought about those parakeets. Mostly, I thought about that anger in Zara's eyes, her set jaw and tight lips. She cared about something, and that was worth everything.

MAMA AND AUNT TABBY came home and left again. On Friday nights, they hit The Roadhouse for margarita pitchers. Mama always said it was their one good time, and she'd met all our daddies there—not that she didn't know them already. Better to say she hooked up with our daddies there, but I hated thinking about my mama that way. I always wished my parents were married, or at least that Mama had married someone, sometime. When your parents are married, you don't have to think, *Did he really like her? Did he just bang her and walk away, and if he did, did she really want me?* Diamond and Jett and I never talked about it, probably 'cause Mama didn't. You don't want to think that you owe your whole existence to someone kinda drunk and horny, or about the cussing your mama did when her period didn't come. We'd never tell Diamond's baby that she wouldn't be there but for a clinic without any appointments. They said Diamond could drive to Virginia. We'd never tell her little girl, *If Aunt Emmy hadn't dropped her savings on a tattoo two months before your mama got knocked up—which your gramma loves to remind her about—then you wouldn't exist.* That baby would figure it out one day. Kids always did.

With Mama and Aunt Tabby gone, my sister didn't have a chance to snitch. I barely saw her, anyway; she was passed out cold when I came in. Sweaty and tired, I took my own nap, dressed, and left for work. Alyssa was on, so it was better than most nights—someone to watch my back. We worked groups of guys together and raked in more money that way.

"How you been, Emmy?" she asked after last call, while we changed out of our dance clothes. "I've seen you all night, and we never had a chance to talk."

"Okay," I told her, 'cause she couldn't know about Zara. "Diamond's a bitch but what else is new?"

Alyssa laughed. She was what my gramma called a generous laugher, and I loved that about her. "Diamond's been bitching since she could talk. I swear her first words were 'I'm telling.' How's she feeling?"

"Same," I said. When Alyssa got knocked up, she went baby-crazy. Everything was "Lucky got a tooth," or "Lucky learned to crawl," or "I gotta take Lucky to his WIC appointment." He was almost a year old, and he'd stolen my best friend. It's weird to say that about a baby, but it's true. Before Alyssa got knocked up, we'd hang out all the time. She'd still smoke up, but only when the baby was asleep, and we had to be real quiet or we'd wake him. Lucky was cute, like every other baby, but he drooled and cried like every other baby, too. Hopefully I'd be out by the time Diamond's came. But my car would die, and I'd be socking away money to fix it, so I'd best plan on some earplugs.

"She pick any names yet?" Alyssa asked.

"She likes Mercedes and Porsche." I screwed my face into a yuck. "I said people already called her white trash, and she told me to shut my mouth."

Alyssa laughed again. "You got any plans for tomorrow?"

"Nah," I said. *I'm gonna see this girl I really like*, I wanted to tell her. Alyssa might not care that bi girls exist, but if I told her I was one of them, she'd think, *Was Emmy looking at me? Does she want to mess around?* She'd hate me after that. Maybe I was wrong, but Alyssa was the best friend I had. I couldn't risk it. We'd known each other since the first day of kindergarten—you don't throw that away, not if you can help it. "You maybe wanna do something Sunday night?" I asked.

"Can't hang out, I'm working," she told me, yanking a shirt over her head. "Lucky needs new shoes."

I should've known it had to do with the baby. Everything had to do with the baby anymore. *You know she'll be busy, Emmy*, Aunt Tabby had told me. *You gotta get used to not seeing her.*

That'll never happen, I said. *She'll always make time. We been friends since we were five.*

Aunt Tabby started to say something else, and Mama laid a hand on her shoulder. *She'll find out*, Mama told her, and that was all. I hated that they turned out right.

IN THE MORNING, I woke up again to Diamond's snoring. Our air conditioner hid the morning sun, so the room was gray and sad, all clumped dirty clothes and tattered posters from my high school years. I left them up 'cause I didn't want the walls bare. That would've been its own kind of loneliness, and I had enough of that in my life. I stumbled into the bathroom and turned on the shower. When I leaned down to take off my shorts, I almost fell.

Black vines climbed my ankles. They twined my calves, tangled behind my knees, and wrapped my thighs before disappearing under my shorts. I yanked my clothes off. Those vines reached my lower belly, and they were identical to Zara's.

They looked like tattoos.

I flashed back to the night before—work, no drinking, no drugs, not unless someone spiked my drink, and if that had happened, I wouldn't remember driving home and dropping into bed. I reached for that memory and found it clear as glass: Diamond snorfling, tripping on a dirty shirt, thinking about Zara and wishing my sister wasn't across the room so I could get myself off. I didn't visit a tattoo parlor, and tats as involved as those vines would've taken hours and hours, not counting a drive to Columbia.

I licked my finger and rubbed my leg. Those vines didn't smear. Panic beat in my chest, a frightened sparrow, and I trembled on the edge of hyperventilating from fear and hyperventilating for fear of hyperventilating. Those marks weren't going away. Those marks were etched on my skin like—I wouldn't think that word. "Breathe," I whispered to myself, and even that simple little word helped, spoken aloud like a spell. I closed my eyes and pictured the safest place I could, that swamp spread around me, all green and growing things. It would smell like honeysuckle. Like Zara—my breath kicked into panting, and I had to start all over again. *You're safe,* I told myself. *You're ten years old, and your gramma is hugging you tight. She's showing you how to bake real cornbread. It tastes sweet and buttery, like a promise, and you believe it. You will always be safe and loved. Breathe.*

I clenched my thighs, squeezed my eyes shut, and remembered Gramma, her cushy chest and warm, sweet smell. She'd say she was fat, but I liked her that way. When I was little, I thought people were only fat if my hands didn't touch when I reached around them. That memory, more than anything else, brought me back. I'd been so sure of my rightness, and so proud, 'cause I came up with that rule myself.

I opened my eyes. The cold tile chilled the soles of my feet. I was alone.

I let my head lean against the wall and thought. Water rushed from the faucet. It seemed like a sure, normal thing, like the cool floor under my hand, or those silk sleepy shorts. Sun leaned through the blinds, high and white, past noon; the bathroom smelled like wet towels left to sit til they molded.

Tattoos didn't just appear. It'd be magic if they did, and magic wasn't real. I'd met a few gothy girls who swore it was, but they'd say, *I cast a money spell and won ten dollars on my scratch-off ticket,* or *I did a love spell and so-and-so slept with me.* They made magic from coincidences and wishful thinking. Miracles, real ones—they're for kids and Bible-bangers. You cling to them when you don't have anything else, and they give you hope in a world dead-set against you.

They said Talitha could do something like magic. When doctors couldn't fix something, and someone got healed anyway, maybe that was a kind of magic, but not this kind. Lower Congaree said Talitha could do lots more than that—summon snakes, talk to ghosts, maybe even kill people. But Lower Congaree lives to sit on porches and spin tales. You can't believe people around here. They think their Power Ball numbers are bound to come up eventually. These days, God's short on miracles, so they look to what they have.

One more time, I spit on my finger and scrubbed at my leg. That ink didn't move, so I rubbed harder. A permanent marker would've dulled. My chest tightened, like something vital crumpling up too small. I rubbed so hard I almost tore my skin, and I couldn't feel those lines at all. They were as smooth as tattoos healed a year before.

If you could get any tattoo, what would it be? Zara had asked.

No contest. I'd get vines like yours. But I could never afford them.

You never know, she'd said. I remembered her smile, how it had curved higher on one side. It'd seemed sweet then, but altogether different now—a little more sinister, like a stranger offering candy. Were those tats supposed to be a gift, a magic one, like something in a fairy tale? Fairy-tale presents came with heavy price tags. If you want the boy, you give the sea witch your voice. If you're born gorgeous, your stepmother tries to murder you. There's always a price, and no matter how good the deal sounds, it's always more than you're willing to pay. Anyway, there is no once-upon-a-time. And even if there was, no handsome prince or princess was coming to my rescue. I'd known that since I was eight.

I rubbed the red spot on my thigh, rubbed it hard enough to curl my skin into little balls. My thigh burned, and when the skin came up I knew those were tattoos. They weren't coming off. They were permanent; they were mine; and they'd happened after I met Zara in that swamp. That meant one of two things was true—either Zara put them there, or the swamp did.

You don't wanna go in that swamp, Talitha told me. *There's no one you wanna meet there, and people come back changed.*

I thought she meant mind-different, not body-different. I examined those vines then, really looked at them. Just like Zara's, they were a real artist's work, all delicate lines and shading. They twisted and curled, folded and crimped—*tendrilled*, that was the vocabulary word. They tendrilled up my legs. They twined my inner thighs, and I'd have remembered that part—thinking about needles there made me wince. I bent my leg up like the cheerleader I'd never been. The vines went all the way around, just as complicated on the back as the front. They were stunning. No artist in Columbia, South Carolina could've done that, not any I knew.

Maybe you oughta be grateful, I thought for a second, then shoved it back. I tried not to love them. But when I climbed on the toilet and looked at my legs in the medicine cabinet mirror, those vines were exactly how I'd have wanted them. That made about as much sense as the tats appearing in the first place. Real life never lives up to imagination.

I couldn't keep them secret. If I wore pants, everyone would ask why, and I had to take my clothes off at work. News would get around. Diamond would hear about them, and she'd tattle like a ten-year-old. I couldn't hide them, not if I wanted to keep my job.

No way in hell was I working in that chicken plant.

I met this girl in the swamp. Her tats appeared on my legs. Not only did it sound insane, if Mama *did* believe me, she'd say, *Well, I told you not to go back there. This is your fault. Maybe you learned your lesson, Emmy Ann.*

I stood up. Sometimes, that's all you can do. I might've been close to hyperventilating, all gasping breath and shaking hands, but life goes on, I guess. Seeing real magic knocked me flat, but you can't stay flat forever. You have to stand up, and you have to get in the shower, and you have to wash your legs and think: *These are mine. My legs didn't have tattoos but now they do. I don't know how that ink got there, but I can't scrub them off, so I have to live with them.*

I washed hard, too. My legs turned red. Soap and water were my last hope, and those vines stayed. I turned off the creaky faucet and snagged a towel from the floor. It had probably sat there for days, but I'd forgotten to grab one from my room. I tried not to smell it. Then I almost laughed. Magic tattoos appeared on my legs, and I worried about stinky towels. No, I corrected myself. Like Zara said, nothing disappears. So nothing just appears, either; those tats came from Zara or the swamp, one or the other. My panic settled into bone-deep fear. Once I wished that swamp would show me something magic. I'd hoped for a bobbing orb or a talking crow. Maybe I wanted those tats, but I didn't want them *that* way.

Mama was gonna lose her mind, and I couldn't do a damn thing about it. I could only hold on and pray. So I threw on some shorts, braced myself, and walked into the storm.

Aunt Tabby was flipping pancakes. Mama hunched at the table with a cup of coffee—you don't want to think about your own mother hungover, but she might've been. "Morning," Jett said, looking up from his scrambled eggs. "Hey! That's some nice ink. When did you get that?"

Mama snapped up. "What ink?" I saw her noticing—her eyes got wide, her mouth dropped open, her coffee cup froze in mid-air. "Emerald Ann Joiner," she said, and that quiet anger was meaner than any yelling. "How fucking much did you spend on that?"

"My friend did it. It didn't cost anything." I dropped to a chair. Maybe the fight would pass quicker if she couldn't see my legs. "And before you ask, I met her at work." While I was changing, I'd ginned up a whole story about how that friend was Lexie Smith, and I'd met her at the club. She was training to be a tattoo artist. You have to know your backstory. If your details don't match, or someone asks a question and you take too long to answer, they'll catch you out for sure. Luckily—for once—the family thought I was too dumb to think up much of anything. *She's not the brightest bulb, but Lord knows she does her best*, Mama would say. I couldn't shoot back, *Well, I'd've done better, but me and Alyssa skipped class to smoke pot in the bathroom.*

"Your friend did it. You gonna tell me you got a kitchen tattoo?" Mama slammed her coffee down so hard that some spilled out. "How many times have I told you—"

"She sterilized everything!" I protested, like it was God's honest truth.

"You think you looked like trash before?" Mama dropped back to that soft, dangerous voice. "You look like you walked outta a cathouse. When I was coming up, the only people with tattoos were whores and sailors, and I don't see a fucking boat."

"Mama—" I started, and my voice had an edge that startled me.

"Don't you even try it," she snapped. "I know what people are gonna think of you. They'll say I raised you wrong. You know that, don't you?" The ugliness started. I knew what she'd say: *You look like a tramp. You look like a slut.* She'd call me every bad thing you could say about a girl, all while Aunt Tabby nodded. Sometimes she'd add, *That's right,* or *Uh-huh,* like Mama was preaching a Sunday sermon.

I wouldn't listen to it again. Instead of shame, anger bloomed in my chest, green and strong and bright. "I know what you're gonna say," I told her. "You can save it. I got these tats and I like 'em. You wanna kick me out like Aunt Tabby kicked out Jackson? Go ahead. I dance. I don't fuck for money, no matter what you say, and at least I don't come home smelling like chicken shit."

Mama stared. There were some things you didn't do, and one of them was talk back.

"Y'all are mad 'cause I want something more than what you got," I said. "Too damn bad."

"Emerald Ann Joiner." Mama breathed my name like a cuss word. "Don't you take that tone with me, girl."

"I'll talk however I want," I told her, and it felt good, righteous and holy. "I'll—"

Diamond wandered in. Mama's shouting probably woke her up. "You know Emmy was in that swamp yesterday, too," she said. "I saw her go back there."

"You did not. When d'you think I got those tattoos done? They took hours and hours. I didn't have time to mess around in the swamp, even if I wanted to."

"Your car was still here." Diamond crossed her arms over that big belly, like impending motherhood lent her an authority I'd never have.

"That's 'cause my friend picked me up!" I had that part ready, too. I knew Diamond would pile on—some people are just that predictable.

"You were out in that swamp again?" Mama's voice rose to a shout. "Goddammit, I told you not to go out there! Didn't Talitha tell you the same thing?"

That question had no right answer—a yes would have her asking why I didn't listen, and no would get me called me a liar. I kept quiet.

"Well?" Mama planted her hands on her hips like I was five years old.

My brave anger withered and died. I could've described the whole scene before it happened—Mama shouting, Aunt Tabby nodding, my brother and sister hoping Mama didn't drag them into it. She'd say Jett was lazy, and Diamond an irresponsible hoochie mama. It would be funny if Mama wasn't serious. She'd say she loved us, but sometimes I wondered. What does love mean? When I was little, I thought it meant feeding someone and giving them clothes. As I got older, I thought maybe there was more to it. Maybe love was listening and holding someone when they were sad. That food-and-clothes thing was part of it, but love meant a whole lot more. It took me a long time to learn that. If that was true—and I knew it was—did anyone love me? Gramma had, but she was gone. No one knew I was bi, and maybe that was my answer. My eyes stung. When I started to cry, Mama said, "You go on and cry your eyes out, Emmy Ann, 'cause you know I'm telling the truth."

Sunshine struggled through the narrow kitchen window, but it promised a glorious summer day. It seemed unfair that Mama ruined such a pretty morning. I wished it was raining, or at least cloudy, but the sun went on shining. It always does. The world never stops for our disasters. That seemed like the most unfair thing of all.

EVENTUALLY, I FLED TO my room. Even Diamond left me alone. I heard them watching something in the living room, a dumb show about rich people being rich. I never understood why everyone gawks at millionaires. Those shows leave you envious and sad, remembering that you're poor and always will be. You wish for more than you've got, and it'll hurt you if you think too hard. Those people, they're only famous 'cause they're rich or weird. No one would make a show about us Joiners. Or maybe they would. The world could learn how to feed five people on food stamps.

I curled on my bed and played games on my phone. If I went into the living room, they'd harass me. If I left the house, they'd say, *Where're you going, Emmy Ann? Don't you get another one of those fucking kitchen tattoos.* I wanted to visit Zara. I never wanted to see her again. Either she'd given me those tats or the swamp had, and either way, I wasn't walking back there again.

I tried to concentrate on Wordscapes. It didn't work. I was staring down real magic. In fairy tales, people accept it as part of the scenery. They never freak out, like magic is something different and wild, like if you look too hard, you'll see the world broke open and bloody at your feet. It could've made me insane if I thought too hard.

I yanked my shorts off and looked at my vines, really looked at them, then stood on my bed and examined them in Diamond's dresser mirror. They twined my legs just like Zara's, straight in my underwear, like a promise of something I might not want to give. Drawing the eye right between my legs, it felt like someone could grab hold of them and climb on up. I twisted around and near about hurt my neck trying to see how they looked from behind. For a snatched moment, I thought they were getting thicker. *They aren't*, I assured myself. *You're not used to seeing them.*

I wasn't. Would I ever be? Under my fingers, they were as smooth as tats done months before. I couldn't decide if they'd earn me more money or less. Some guys hated tats. Mostly, though, gothy ones could get away with it. But whatever they were, however they'd appeared, those vines were stunning, art someone would pay thousands and thousands for. *I'd get vines like yours. But I could never afford them.*

I fucking loved them. Dropping to my bed, I curled up. It was too much to think about, too scary. So what if I loved them? They were magic. Gifts were never free. If people gave you something, you owed them something in return. That's how the world worked. It always had. "Lookit all those presents, Emmy Ann," Mama always said on Christmas, when one church or another dropped off gifts. "You better do well in school and make me think you deserve them."

"Yes, ma'am," I'd reply. As tears rose, the Christmas lights would go blurry. Those presents weren't presents at all. They were promises, agreements: *You give me this, and I'll give you that.*

You can waste a whole day on your phone. You don't even have to try.

When I finally got ready for work, Mama and Aunt Tabby were gone. On the saggy, secondhand couch, Diamond and Jett were watching one of those shows about naked people stranded on an island. "Where're you going?" my sister asked. Her eyes didn't move from the TV, all naked butts, and her hand didn't leave that bag of chips. Apparently, if they put you on prime time, it's okay to take off your clothes.

"You know damn well where I'm going," I said.

Diamond snorted. She'd only spoken up so she could start a fight. "You're gonna go shake your ass for money, that's what you're gonna do."

Jett sank lower. He hated when we fought, and he hated when they talked about my job. I ignored Diamond and grabbed a banana from the kitchen table.

She couldn't let me go that easy. "How d'you think Jett feels when the guys at school say they saw you naked?"

"They don't—" Jett started, then shut up. He never could stand up to her.

I peeled my banana and took a bite, but I couldn't taste it. I was tired of taking shit from her. I refused to pluck dead chickens til my hands ached. *You're doing great, Emmy,* they should've said. *You don't have much, but you use what you got.* I was gonna get myself outta that house, maybe even that town. I didn't know where I'd go, but it'd be bigger, brighter, full of people who never did or said a boring thing. There would be lesbians, and trans people, and bi people and gay people and everyone in between. They'd hold hands on the street, and people would smile. I'd be more than they ever thought I could be, more than that airless box they squished me into. Light cracked through my broken places then. Call it strength, maybe, a power twining around my ribs and tangling my chest. Suddenly, I wanted to smash life open. I wanted to leave it red and weeping at my feet.

"Least I'm not pregnant," I told Diamond. "Dancing lasts one night, and pays money besides. You'll be stuck with that baby for eighteen years. You still wanna make me ashamed? See how it feels in four months when you're digging through the couch cushions for diaper money."

Her hand went over her belly. "It's not gonna be like that," my sister said, and a little bit of that mean turned scared. "It's not."

"Uh-huh." They could see my new tattoos and I didn't care. "Why's it not gonna be like that? 'Cause you're getting diapers from the food bank? Jett's smart enough to wrap it up, and he's only fifteen. You were too stupid to do it when you were twenty-three. Now you're making the rest of us pay for it. Call me a whore if you want, but you're the one who got in trouble for fucking." I spoke in the same cold, angry voice Mama used on me.

"Shut up," Diamond said, her eyes filling. "Stop it, Emmy Ann."

"No, if I stop it you'll call me a whore again," I snapped back. The TV babbled on, people trying to make do when they had nothing left. "Good for you for keeping that baby, if that's what you wanted. I mean it, too. But don't call me names for making my own choices."

"You go to hell." She swiped at her face. "You know I didn't want a baby."

"Well, your choices got you one," I said. "And I'm sorry for that. But don't take it out on me. Don't take it out on Jett, either, 'cause as soon as I walk outta here, that's what you're gonna try."

Thank you, Jett mouthed.

"You're welcome," I told him. Grabbing my purse, I picked up my keys and left.

All that anger had finally come out, like I knew it would one day. I always worried I'd choke on it. *You did good, Emerald*, I imagined Zara saying. *You did exactly right.* Then I remembered I'd never tell her about it, and all that strength drained away. Sadness hunched in its place. Zara knew I liked girls. When I was with her, I didn't have to pretend.

It didn't matter. Those tattoos had appeared overnight, and I'd best stay away from her, stay away from that swamp. Magic scared me, and even if it didn't, I'd owe a price I could never pay. Zara might try to collect it, and I didn't want to think about what that might mean.

If I cried, I'd ruin my makeup, so I counted breaths instead. When I turned onto the highway, the swamp closed in, all green, braided vines. Even through the rushing wind, I heard its cicadas humming. Damn Zara. I wasn't in love with her, I told myself. You can't be in love with a person you saw twice in your life. But if I had to name that feeling, the word *love* came closest.

I pulled into the club's dust-dry parking lot. *Breathe*, I ordered myself. *Take two deep breaths and forget about it.* I'd done that when my daddy left. Five years old, I'd been hiding around the living room corner when he slammed out our front door. Mama thumped onto the couch and fell into strangling sobs that could've torn me open like a rag doll. *You can't cry*, I'd thought then. *Be sad for two deep breaths, then forget about it.* Maybe I'd heard that on one of Mama's shows, those endless soap operas with people always dying and fighting and poisoning each other. So I took two shuddery breaths and set it aside. I'd been startled at how well it worked. Kids figure out how to survive, I guess. Their insides fray, and they learn to hide the tattered places.

I drew two deep breaths, then walked across that hot, gritty parking lot. As usual, guys hung around the club's black door. One was poking through the ashtray and pretending not to. He couldn't afford cigarettes, so he was smoking someone else's butts.

"Hey, honey," said a skeletal guy with too much acne. "What're you up to tonight?"

"Dancing," I replied as I passed.

He leaned on the dirty wall. "Maybe you wanna go home with me instead."

"Maybe I don't fuck methheads," I shot back. Usually I'd only think something like that, and it startled me as much as him.

His friend laughed. I pushed the door open and stepped from day to that strange, timeless night. Mirrors reflected the Christmas lights, someone's sad ideas of stars. No one was dancing. Bass thumped like a second heartbeat, and a few men scattered the chained-down tables. No girls were on yet, but they would be soon.

I caught Noah's face as he saw my tats. His nose wrinkled, and his forehead furrowed, and he ducked down fast, maybe hoping I wouldn't see. He hated them. Instead of sagging, though, I squared my shoulders. They weren't his, and they weren't *for* him. They weren't for anyone. I hadn't done them, but I'd asked for them, and they were mine. I loved them.

"What d'you think of the tats?" I asked, sliding onto a barstool.

He smiled, but it didn't reach his eyes. You can always tell a fake smile. I'd seen too many of them. "I like them if you like them," he told me.

"Thanks," I said, and he slid me a Coke. "A friend of mine did 'em."

"Be careful." He held up a finger to a customer: *I'll be there in a sec.* "If you just got them done, they'll be tender today. Don't mess with that."

I was that girl who followed all the aftercare instructions. I washed new tats three times a day, patted them dry, and rubbed them with Desitin. If those vines were new, I'd have been wrapped in plastic-y bandages, laid up in the air conditioning, and sure as hell not about to dance. "I'll be careful," I told Noah.

"You don't wanna scar 'em." Noah fussed below the bar, like I might see too much in his face if he stood up. "Who did those? I've been looking for a good artist."

"My friend Lexie's an apprentice." I scrunched up my nose. "She lives down in Miami. Left just before I came in today." I had to pick somewhere far away, too far for him to travel.

"Too bad." He gave me one of those grins that don't quite sit straight. "Well, lemme know if you need some aspirin for them, okay? Helps take down inflammation."

"I will," I said. Hefting my bag, I threaded backstage. I could feel all those men watching me. They were wondering what I'd look like naked. *Let them look*, I thought. *Let them see what they're gonna pay for.* I strode slower, from my hips, and if they weren't staring at my ass before, they watched then. In heels, covered in long, winding vines, my legs looked a million miles long. I imagined them with those jean shorts that barely covered my ass, and I wished Zara could see. Our legs would've looked so pretty tangled together. I'd missed seeing her. She would've waited at our spot all afternoon. *Two deep breaths*, I told myself as I pictured her worrying, then getting up and walking home alone. *Two deep breaths, Emmy.* Even if I wanted to forget her, those tattoos would never let me.

Alyssa squealed when I stepped into the dressing room—trust her to notice right away. "Oh my God, when did you get *those* done?" she asked. "Emmy, those are gorgeous!"

"Thanks," I said, and we went through the who-did-those, she's-from-Miami talk. I told Alyssa the artist was a friend of Jackson's friend. 'Cause of the pot dealing, she stayed away from him; they'd take Lucky if she got caught near a dealer.

At the bottom of my bag, I found those booty shorts I never dared to wear, black with shiny-buckled garters. When I pulled them out, Alyssa asked, "Are you gonna wear *them*? Emmy, that'll look awesome."

"Yeah," I said, and after I tied on a black bikini top, I added a body harness I'd never tried, either. The collar strapped around my neck, and a chain led to the buckle below my boobs. I'd always wanted to try it, but I never quite had the courage.

"It looks killer, but are you sure it'll be okay rubbing those new tats?" Alyssa turned around, and I tied her string bikini.

"They'll be fine. I lotioned them up real well, and the girl who did them said they'd be okay." I glanced in the mirror. Vines arched just above my shorts and dipped down again. I'd never wear garters again, at least not any that started at my ankles. My legs were stunning on their own.

Alyssa went out first. When she finished, the DJ started Nine Inch Nails's "Starfuckers, Inc.," and I strode onstage. Instead of staring into the dark, I focused on the men next to the stage. Then I planted my back against the pole and grabbed above my head. As the lyrics kicked in, I squatted down, hands sliding with me, then back up, and I was gone. For once I didn't think about what those men were thinking, or if I danced well, or how much I wished for an audience of girls. *Let them want what they can't have*, I thought. *Let them wish for it, and let them pay for those wishes.* Spinning and twisting, I lost myself in that dance. Guys tucked money in my harness, in my garters. When I crouched on the edge of the stage, they whispered in my ear, and I laughed.

"Let's grab a room," said an older guy. I might've recognized him, maybe someone's dad. It should've icked me out.

"Sure, honey," I said.

I spent most of the night drinking wine with him—the first time I drank at work—in one of those curtained boxes that count as private rooms. Of course, he asked if I'd do more than dance. "That's illegal," I laughed, and he didn't bring it up again. Those rooms cost a hundred an hour—twenty-five to the house, seventy-five to me. I walked outta there with three hundred dollars and two hours left before closing. I hadn't thought of Zara the whole time. I might've been more grateful for that than the money.

"Good job," Noah said afterward, pushing a Coke in my direction.

"Thanks," I told him.

"Great dance, earlier. If I'd've been in the front row, you'd've taken all my money." He gave me a crooked grin. I smiled back. If he wasn't my boss, I might've flirted back.

"I think I cleaned a few of them out," I replied, absolutely serious. When I checked my thong after that dance, I found a twenty.

"You sure you don't want any rum in that?" He gestured at my drink.

"Nah," I said. "I'm about to hit the floor."

"Your car running okay?" Alana's "Get Low" kicked on, and Noah leaned his elbows on the bar. "It was making a funny noise when you pulled out the other night. I can always pick you up, y'know? Don't drive something that might get you hurt." Noah's brown hair looked messier than usual, and under the Christmas lights, his eyes were wide and dark. He was cute, if you were into that.

"Thanks," I said, draining the rest of my drink. "Imma get dancing. Lemme know if you need anything." I left the empty Coke on the bar. My Nissan had bald tires and a wonky air conditioner; God only knew what was wrong under the hood. I expected it to die every time I stuck the key in. Noah was so sweet. Hopefully I wouldn't need his offer, but if I did, it'd keep me outta that chicken plant.

Back on the floor, I plopped down next to some lonely guys and scored some dances. About an hour later, I kissed one on the cheek and hopped to the floor. After hustling my ass off, I was ready for a bathroom trip and a breather. The day had sunken too late or too early, depending on your point of view, and the club was dropping into that sad hour of solo guys and hard drinkers, men who'd whisper and sag over their liquor. They'd want to talk about their emptiness instead of buying dances. Sometimes, they'd cry. When that happened, I'd pat their backs and tell them it wasn't that bad, not really. I was always lying.

"Hey." A hand closed over my wrist. The Wheeler kid's breath smelled worse than before. "Where you going, girl?"

I shook him off. "What, you gonna wait at the door like a creeper and try to ambush me again?" I spoke loud over the music, loud so guys nearby could hear. "Don't touch me, you sick-ass motherfucker."

A guy at a nearby table stood. His chair screeched over the sticky floor like a challenge, and he had to be six-three, all beefed-out football muscle. "Is this guy bothering you, ma'am?"

"He sure as hell was bothering her the other night." Noah loomed over the Wheeler kid, who shrank into his seat. He was the type of guy who bullied women when he could get away with it, but backed down like a kicked dog when he couldn't. I knew that type. They made up two-thirds of the men in Lower Congaree.

"He's not bothering me anymore," I told Noah. "Thanks. He was just leaving, I think." Then I smiled at the big guy. "I'll be right back, sweetie. Save me a spot on your lap."

"You heard her," Noah said as I walked away. "Get the fuck out or I'll make you wish you had. And don't you wait around in that parking lot, Isaac. I'll put your head through this table if something happens to her, and I'll tell your preacher daddy why I did it, too."

It was that easy. I'd never known, or maybe I'd been too scared to try it. That power bloomed between my ribs again, the feeling I had when I told off Diamond. That night, I left with four hundred and fifty dollars, double what I usually pulled in, and I kissed Noah's cheek as he walked me out.

"Thanks again," I told him.

"Be safe, Emmy," he replied, a hand resting on my shoulder. "Lemme know if anyone bothers you."

He'd never called me Emmy before. My car started, and I waved as I drove out. I might not have had Zara, but someone was watching my back. That lost, sad ache settled again. I wished I could tell Zara about that night. *I was brave*, I'd have said. *They loved my tats, and I wasn't scared.*

You should always be that brave, she'd say. *It wasn't the tattoos. It was you, Emerald.*

She'd touch my cheek, and I'd believe it.

I WAS OFF SUNDAY. Everyone else went to church, even Jett—Mama and Aunt Tabby liked the Holiness church. I stopped going the first time Mama spoke in tongues. Shouting nonsense, she fell down on the floor, and even though it looked like another flavor of normal there, I wanted to die from the shame of it. It sort of broke my heart at the same time, too. Mama speaking in tongues was a kind of wishful thinking, not that she necessarily faked it. Those people wanted God to touch them so badly that they thought he actually had. I didn't believe Jesus and his angels watched us from heaven. If he did, I hated him. Think of all that power. He wouldn't even drop in to fix Mama's back, bent up and hurting from a dozen years of plucking chickens. He let people die, and hurt little kids, and do all the terrible things that people do so often they blend into the scenery. He could've fixed it. So like hell was I watching Mama fall down and claim he was behind it all.

If Jesus was real, he was sending me to hell. Why go to church? The old people whispered about me behind their hands, and I could read it on their faces: *Emmy Ann Joiner has sex for money.* Better to stay home alone, wishing for something to believe in.

After breakfast, I wandered to the front porch for a smoke. Everything seemed motionless, stuck in heat-soaked stillness. I felt like I was waiting for the world to begin again. Lighting a cigarette, I slumped in a dry-rotted lawn chair. I could've been the last person on Earth.

I thought about that, what I'd do if I was totally alone, how I'd break into the stores and try on all the clothes, then make myself filet mignon for dinner. I'd never had it, but it sounded nice. I was still thinking about that when an old orange car drove around the corner. That movement felt like a miracle. It pulled into the drive, and Talitha rolled down the window farther. Wind had blown her dark hair messy. She didn't wear makeup, but she didn't need any.

"Hey, Emmy!" she called. "Tell your mama I stopped by, will you?"

"You can stay til she comes," I said, 'cause it was the polite thing to do. Mama would be home in about half an hour. I didn't want to spend my morning with Talitha Merle, but it didn't look like I had a choice. "You want a smoke?"

She turned off the car and climbed out. "Yeah," she replied. "I haven't had one in a long time." I handed her a cigarette, and she took the other rickety chair. "Damn, but this is good," she said. "Nothing like smoking outside on a hot summer morning."

She was right, though I'd never put it into words. There was something good about that stillness, watching those trees hang motionless and smoking my first cigarette of the day.

"Nice tats," Talitha told me. "When did you get those?"

"The other day," I replied. It wasn't a lie.

She squinted. "They look real healed up."

"Guess so." There wasn't much else I could say. Those tats looked real healed up 'cause no one had stuck needles in me. Maybe I was lucky, maybe cursed. I'd managed not to think about it that morning.

"Huh." Talitha didn't say anything else, like she'd decided to let me keep my secrets.

We were alone. If I didn't have enough courage to ask then, I never would. The only bi girl I'd ever met was Zara. I wondered if there was an underground place to go, or a code so secret it wasn't on the internet. I'd looked. *How do you know*, I wanted to ask. *And once you know, how do you ask if she likes you?* "I don't wanna bring up anything bad," I said carefully. "But Mama and Aunt Tabby were talking one time, and they said that even though you're married now, you went out with girls before."

Talitha glanced at me quick, surprised, then smiled. "Never tried to keep it a secret. You too, huh?"

My eyes must've gone deer-in-the-headlights. She laughed. "Don't worry," she told me. "I only knew 'cause you mentioned it. I'm right, aren't I?"

"Don't tell, please?" I asked. She'd scared me for a moment, like I had it written on me and everyone could see. "Mama would lose her mind. It's one thing if it's you and another if it's her own daughter."

"Lord, I know what that's like." Talitha looked at the trees across the road, a dark, unknowable tangle. "I didn't go out with a girl til my mama passed." She seemed to think for a while, like she was remembering a girl, or maybe remembering that sick, trapped feeling, like being held underwater. "You ever gone out with a girl?" she asked eventually.

Talitha would know if I was lying. "Maybe," I said. "I don't know. I kissed her."

"Did you like her?" she asked.

I watched those tall, still trees. The swamp stretched beyond them—the whole town twined through swampland. When it rained too hard, roads flooded, and little creeks churned into angry rivers. We lived in it and with it. Maybe it fucked with us some, having that strange place so close. I wondered if life was different away from it. Maybe there were small differences I'd never notice unless I left. "The girl I kissed?" I said finally. "Yeah. I liked her a whole lot. They wouldn't believe me, though. They'd say I was fooling around and it wasn't serious, 'cause she's a girl."

"Did you want it to be serious?" Talitha asked.

"I think so," I replied. "Yeah. I think I did." I wanted it more than anything. I wanted to wake up next to Zara, all soft edges and curves. Morning sun would warm my face while I nuzzled into her neck. The tiny hairs there would tickle my nose, and she'd smell like home.

"What was the girl like?" Maybe Talitha was studying me. I didn't look.

"Pretty," I said right away. Now that we were talking, something about Talitha inspired trust, like I could hand her all my secrets. "But she was sweet, too. She listened. And she made me feel like I could be more than I was, y'know? More than other people see. They all think I have sex for money." I spit it like a curse. Suddenly my cigarette tasted ashy and bitter-sick. I mashed it under my flip-flop.

"I know they give you a hard time for dancing," Talitha said. "Did she?"

I was grateful she'd said dancing, not stripping. "No," I replied. "She knew, and she didn't care."

Talitha drew a long puff on her cigarette, then breathed out a rolling cloud of smoke. "So that girl was kind and she liked you for who you are. I should smack you silly. Why the hell did you let her go?"

"It's a long story," I said. "I sorta had to."

"No good reason for letting go of someone who sees you and loves you anyway." Talitha spoke as seriously as Mama's preacher, like I'd skipped church and found it waiting on the front porch.

I sagged, and my chair creaked under me. It'd fall apart soon. My car, the house—they'd fall apart, too. Sometimes it felt like the whole world was tumbling down, and I couldn't do a damn thing to stop it. "I had a good reason for letting her go."

The swamp seemed wrapped in quiet, like it was waiting for us to speak. I drank some water and lit another cigarette.

Talitha snagged another from my pack. "I went out with Charlotte Price for a few months," she said. "Long time back. She's married to Estlin Lanier now—y'know, the big-shot lawyer. Three kids." A little smile crept up her cheeks again. "She probably forgot all about me by now. Trust me, I remember her. But part of me was always shut off when we were together. She didn't want to hear about my life. She'd say it scared her. 'Don't talk about the people who need your help,' she'd tell me. If I was mixing up herbs for someone, she'd walk out. 'I don't wanna know what it's for,' she said once.

"So I eventually told her it wasn't working out. You can't be with someone who doesn't accept all of you. And when someone does, you hold on for dear life, Emmy. Those people are few and far between, and you don't let them go."

"I had to." My throat started to close, and my chest hurt. I wanted to tell her everything, but I didn't dare. *I told you so*, she'd say. *You don't mess with some things. You got yourself into this, and you can get yourself out.* That's what Mama would've said if she believed me. She wouldn't. I wouldn't have believed me either, so I couldn't hold it against her.

We quieted again. There was no wind, no birds, no squirrels dashing through their everyday business. I drew on my cigarette and concentrated on that ashy burn. It filled my lungs, and when I breathed it out, the smoke rolled up and away, one movement in all that motionless, stretched time.

"Huh," Talitha said again. "Does that girl have anything to do with your new tats? I'm sure as the day is long you didn't sit for 'em. They're too healed up—anyway, I saw your legs on Thursday, and I'd've noticed those tattoos."

I froze. Cigarette smoke hazed into the sky, and I thought about running. I thought about leaving Talitha there on that porch, slamming the door and hiding in my room. She'd have told Mama. I never should've offered her a cigarette.

But Talitha wasn't done. "You smell like magic, girl. It about slapped me in the face when I came up on this porch. You wanna tell me what's going on?"

"Nothing," I managed. "I don't know what you're talking about."

"Uh-huh." Talitha leaned back in her chair. I swear I felt her looking at me. "You gonna tell me you aren't up to some kinda magic?"

"No," I told her. Not a lie—I hadn't done the magic. Zara had. I dropped my cigarette and ground it out. I still had about half of it left, but my heart beat too hard, and I was almost dizzy.

"Emmy, you can tell me the truth." Talitha's voice turned kind—almost like she wanted to help. But no one ever helped, and she wasn't gonna lure me into that game. The sooner you learn that you're on your own, the better.

"Look, it's not every day that magic pops up in your life," she said after a long, settling silence. "If you want help, I'm here."

"Is it bad magic?" The question came before I could stop it. If she could tell me, I wanted to know.

Talitha nodded like she expected that question. "People talk about white magic and black magic all the time. Everyone's either Glinda the Good Witch or a straight-out Satanist. But there's no such thing as all-good or all-bad. Magic's the ultimate gray area, honey. Was it meant with kindness or malice? Does it make you do bad things?"

"No," I said. "I told someone I wanted these tats and could never afford them."

"There's your answer, then." Talitha's chair creaked as she got up. "Tell your mama I stopped by."

"I will," I said. "But—"

"No buts, Emmy." Talitha swished through the brown grass, sad and parched with summer, then climbed into her car. "You find that girl again, you hear me? She accepts you. You got anyone else who does that?"

"Other than you?" I asked, and she tipped me a wave as she pulled out. I went into the house. I didn't have anybody, not really. Life was lonely, but I figured everyone was lonely most of the time, so why not me? *Hold on for dear life, Emmy. Those people are few and far between, and you don't let them go.*

Maybe I had a chance at something. I turned on the shower. Those tattoos were beautiful. Maybe they were magic, but Zara had handed that magic to me. I didn't even believe in it, or at least I hadn't. It didn't matter. Zara knew who I was, and that was the best magic of all.

And so what if she could do things like that? Maybe people could, like Talitha, and I'd just never seen it. The whole world seemed bigger than I'd ever imagined then, huge and full of secrets. If Zara could paint tattoos on my legs, she could find me.

I showered, dressed, and walked into the swamp.

BIRDS WHISTLED IN THE trees, and humidity hugged me close. The greens seemed brighter, and vines hung like birthday-banners. That swamp didn't seem like the same gray place surrounding our school playground, the woods kids pointed to and said, "You'll disappear if you go back there." Little birds flitted from branch to branch. Somewhere, a woodpecker drummed, and small creatures rummaged through the underbrush. Everything was alive and vivid, like I'd left a dull world behind and stepped into technicolor. I felt like Dorothy walking into Oz.

"You're here!" Zara bounced to her feet and threw her arms around me. I nuzzled into her neck and breathed her in. "Why didn't you come yesterday? I was so worried."

I tried not to think about that, about her waiting and watching the trail. At every sound, she'd have snapped up, looking and hoping. I've waited like that too many times. You sit and hope, and slowly, that hope turns to sadness. The knowledge comes bit by bit until you see it: Whatever you're waiting for, it's not coming, and that last little bit of hope dries up. You feel it crumbling, like a plant dying on a windowsill, leaves curling and brown. I hate that feeling more than almost any other.

"I was scared," I said. My lips brushed Zara's coppery neck. I'd cry if I imagined her waiting for me. "I woke up with tattoos, and it freaked me out, y'know?"

"You like them, right?" She drew back, and my arms went achingly empty. We sat down. "You said you wanted them. You said they'd make you feel more like you. I thought . . ." Blinking hard, she trailed off. "I'm sorry."

"I love them," I said quickly. "It was sweet of you. I just didn't expect it. Then I talked to someone, and she told me—well, she told me if I thought they were a gift, then they weren't bad. She said people who accept you are few and far between, and you need to hold on to them."

"I wanted you to have something beautiful." Zara's dark eyes were big, serious, maybe still close to tears. "Move your legs and let me see."

Obediently, I scooted over and stretched out, almost sighing at the cool moss pressing my legs. I could've stretched out and watched the leaves ruffle above us.

"Oooh." Zara traced my calf, and my breath caught. "Those look even better than mine."

She laid her head on my shoulder. It felt right, satisfying, like tossing a rock in the water and hearing its deep plop.

"The guys at work liked them," I said. "I bitched one out last night. When it happened I thought, 'Zara would be proud of me.'" Then I told her all the things I'd wanted to say—I told her about Mama, and my fight with Diamond, and Isaac Wheeler and how much money I'd made at work. "It almost felt like the tattoos helped," I said. "But how did you do them?"

Zara's laugh rippled through the quiet forest. "I just *did it*, Emerald. There's no how. You could do it if you believed you could."

"I don't think so," I said. "I would've figured it out by now."

"Nah," she told me. "People don't. They think magic—if that's what you want to call it—they think it's for books and stories. They never realize they're holding it in their hands." Zara stretched her legs out with mine, and they looked pretty together, as pretty as I'd hoped. "I like that," she said. "We match. It's kind of hot, too."

"I was picturing that," I admitted. "I was thinking how hot they would look next to each other? I don't know why it's so hot." I blushed then. It probably wasn't the right thing to say.

"They do look pretty." Zara wiggled her bare toes. "You wanna see something?"

"Uh, sure," I said, and she jumped to her feet. "We have to walk a little bit," she told me, pulling me up and bounding down the trail. "It's not far, though. You won't believe it. I saw it on the way here."

Zara held my hand, and she moved fast, a ground-covering stride that said she was used to hikes. Trumpet vines twined up cypress trunks; small birds flitted from branch to branch. The swamp was alive, summer-green, swelling and sprouting. "Are we going to your house?" I asked. "I'd love to see your place."

"Not my house," she said, but offered nothing else.

"You said you live near here, right?" She tugged me along, and I trotted to keep up. "What road?"

"Middle of nowhere," Zara told me promptly. "It's complicated. It's not my house."

She must've been staying with someone. Maybe it embarrassed her. I wouldn't want to bring Zara to my house, so I understood that. She'd see the sagged siding, the dirty walls, the unmown grass. Taken together, the battered house and beat-down cars looked more like laziness than poverty, but we couldn't help it. Time and energy were in short supply at my house. We didn't have a lawnmower, and the landlord didn't give a shit about snakes in the front yard; if you don't have a washer and dryer, dirty clothes pile up—laundromats are sad places, all meth heads and old ladies with trembling lips. The first will steal your quarters. The second will moan about their grandchildren never visiting and late social security checks. Laundromats are a concentration of human misery, like the WIC office, all people life left behind. You wouldn't go there if you had a choice, and we put it off as long as possible. Our kitchen needed a scrub-down; eventually, Mama would holler at Jett to clean the bathroom. I'd help him scrape caked-up mold from the tiles. Our house reeked of good enough, of tired and tired of. Zara didn't need to see it. Maybe her house was the same way.

Zara stopped at a stream, wide and mazy. Curving through the cypress-forest like a sleepy country highway, it could've sheltered anything—alligator, catfish, gar as long as my leg. "We need to cross this creek," she said, hiking her dress to her thighs. Her tats were beautiful then, black on her brown skin, and a little thrill bubbled in my tummy. Mine probably looked just as good.

"Is it deep?" I eyed the molasses-slow water, black with tannin. I couldn't see the bottom.

"Nah. Nothing in there will bother you, either, so don't go all squicky on me." Her smile bloomed like a sunrise, and she stepped in. Nose wrinkled, I splashed after her. Dark water splashed my short-shorts. I followed close behind her, careful not to step in any holes. I didn't want to get wet, but the water was blessedly cool, and once I waded in, I resisted sinking down to my neck. I could've stayed in that stream all day. If I'd have lingered, floated on my back and watched the branches arching above, the water would whisper secrets in my ears. It would hold me like my grandmother's hugs, welcomed me, like it had waited for me to wade in.

Zara slipped up the bank and ducked behind a bush. "It's right up there," she whispered. "You have to be very quiet. He knows me, but he'll fly away from you." She pointed. Around an upstream bend, an egret picked through the shallows. White-plumed, yellow-legged, he peered at the water like he was reading a book. I drew a sharp breath. I'd never seen one so big.

"How can you know an egret?" I asked.

"Shh," she hissed.

The enormous bird picked through the shallows. All tensile strength, he stabbed into the water, came up with a fish, and took it down like a sword-swallower. I gasped.

"Hush," Zara told me. "If you're quiet, he'll stick around."

And he did. We crouched, silent, for almost half an hour as he poked through that creek.

After three more fish, he shrugged water from his feathers, kicked off the bottom, and flew soundlessly downstream.

"He was beautiful," I told Zara. In his silent wake, speaking seemed sacrilegious, like a cuss word in church.

Zara gazed after him. "The Indians here, before white people came, they kept tame cranes. Did you know that? The cranes flew away when smallpox came, and the people died so quick no one could bury them. Their bodies sank into the swamp." She drew a long, shuddery breath. "They were famous for their cranes. They wandered the village like pets. They're gone now. All of it's gone. We lost so much." She turned to me, expression fierce. "You have no idea, Emerald. None. Can you imagine the quiet? Happy quiet, people living with the land and the land living with them." She pronounced a word I didn't understand.

"What was that?" I asked, straightening up. My back had crinked. The swamp returned to its usual chorus, or maybe I just noticed it again.

She pronounced the word again. "It was their word that meant 'living together with the land.'"

"You mean from the Congaree Indians?" I asked. "When we learned about them in sixth grade, they said their language was gone."

Zara strode back to the stream and clambered down the bank. She used the cypress knees like stepping stones. "They were wrong," she told me, "and don't call them 'Congaree.' That was what the Catawba called them, not what they called themselves."

I wanted to ask what name they used. But Zara's mouth had hardened to a thin white line, and I didn't want to poke that anger. "What'd I do?" I asked, all caution.

"Nothing." She dropped into the stream, everything but her head underwater. "Sorry. I get mad about the Indians, y'know? A whole culture gone. No one thinks about them anymore."

I sank into the stream. That water held me like a whispered mercy. I closed my eyes and floated. Maybe I should've been afraid. People said there were cottonmouths thick as a thigh in that swamp, gators like compact cars, catfish the size of VW Bugs—they're always the size of VW Bugs; ask anyone for a big-fish catfish story, and they'll use that exact phrase. I don't know if they're really that huge, or if it's just a thing people say. I always wondered. So I should've been scared to float in that water. But it felt kind. *The stream won't let anything hurt me*, I thought, which was stupid, but there you go.

So we swam, soaking our clothes. Zara told me more about the Indians then. "How d'you know all this?" I asked.

"I just do," she told me, then talked about their skill with a spear. I listened. That was all she wanted, maybe—a witness, a listener, someone to shoulder their story and gather that sadness close. I understood that. So many times, I craved that understanding. When bad things happen, you want someone to see your hurt; lonely sadness is the worst kind. When kids laughed at my knock-off shoes, when they poked fun at my free lunches, when they called my family low-life trash, Mama would say, "Ignore them. They're jealous." *Of what*, I'd want to ask. *Nobody's jealous of being poor.* Only Alyssa would listen, and she didn't have a lot of patience for it. "Look on the good side, Emmy," she'd say. "Least you got sneakers and lunch. Plenty of people, they don't." *So where are they?* I'd want to say. *'Cause there sure as hell aren't many people in Lower Congaree poorer than me.*

So I listened to Zara. The swamp seemed to sing a counterpart to her words, and even the cypresses felt sadder, grayer, like they'd lost something they could never find again. Some of those trees were old enough to have seen those forgotten Indians. When Zara cried, I waded over and hugged her. Her head rested on my shoulder, and her tears smeared my neck. I wanted to tell her it was okay. I couldn't. It would never be okay. Something beautiful was gone forever.

When her tears went down to sniffles, she lifted her head. "I should get going," she told me.

"How can I get in touch with you?" I asked. "I mean, once I go home. We could text."

"I'll see you tomorrow," she said, scrambling up the bank. Mud smeared her pretty tattoos, but she didn't bother to wipe it off. "Can you come tomorrow? I promise not to be so sad. I'll show you something else. You'll like it. Swear."

"Yeah," I said. "I can come tomorrow." Either Zara didn't want to talk to me outside the swamp, or she wasn't ready. I had to be patient, maybe. People at home probably didn't know she liked girls.

"I'll see you then," she told me. "You know the way back?"

"Same time, same place?" I said. "Except—well—" I chose my words carefully, 'cause I didn't want her to think I was ashamed. "They don't know I come out here. My mama tells me not to, and she gets mad if she catches me. Is there anywhere else—"

"Yeah," she said. "You can drive, right? Drive to that place all the kids go to make out and take the north trail. I'll meet you about a mile in, at the stream bend." And she bounded away, that same quick stride.

When I reached home, I walked in the front door instead of the back. Mama was already making Sunday dinner, spaghetti and store-bought meatballs. Frozen ones were cheaper than hamburger meat. "Hey," I said to her and Jett. "My friend Amber and I went to the swimming hole. How was church?"

Mama fixed a beady eye on me. "Why didn't you take a goddamn bathing suit? Get in there and change. You're dripping all over the floor, Emmy Ann."

Ducking into the bedroom, I hid a secret smile. They had no idea.

In the morning, I drove to the Lot and hiked out. Mosquitoes had stopped bothering me; I didn't know if they weren't biting or I was used to them. Zara and I hugged when we met, then she bounced down the trail. "C'mon," she urged. "The surprise isn't far."

But it was, about three miles of far, but I didn't complain. Finally, she led me off the trail and slipped behind a bush. "Be really, really quiet," she said when I dropped next to her. "No one knows these are back here, and *you can't tell anyone*, Emerald. Swear."

"I swear," I told her solemnly, and hooked my pinkie into hers.

"Why'd you do that?" In the deep shade, she stared at our linked pinkies like I'd done something strange.

"Pinkie swear," I said, studying her wrinkled nose and creased forehead. Zara had the cutest confused face. "Didn't you pinkie swear when you were a kid?"

"Nah." She pointed to a craggy dead tree. "Now hush. It'll come back in a second."

Five minutes later, a bird landed on a splintery branch. Red-headed, black-bodied, it reminded me of those old Woody Woodpecker cartoons. I'd never seen anything like it; the bird was as big as a crow, bright-eyed. Brambles brushed my face as I crept closer.

"Ivory-billed woodpecker," Zara whispered.

"They're extinct!" I hissed.

"So everyone thinks." She flashed a wicked grin. Tears pricked my eyes. Not lost at all, but the swamp's best secret.

On Tuesday, Zara showed me the oldest cypress in the state. "It's older than Shakespeare," she said, and one more time, I almost cried. Instead, I rested my palm on its smooth bark. *Hello,* I said to it. *Thank you for still being here.*

A flush of love overwhelmed me, sure as my gramma's hug. Zara rested her head against its rough trunk. "Think of the stories it has," she said.

"I wish I could hear them." I stroked its bark, cracked as mud parched by sunshine.

Zara touched my cheek. "Maybe you'll hear them someday," she told me, and it didn't feel crazy, but sweet.

On Wednesday, my eyes popped, and I cowered in the brush as an albino gator heaved from the muck. It really was as big as a compact car, a swamp-giant, white and red-eyed and strange. "He won't hurt you," Zara whispered. "He's blind, and he doesn't like to leave the water."

When the gator sank again, I bolted. Brush crashed; birds shouted; legs pumping, I ran like the devil was chasing me. Mud splashed my thighs as I crashed through puddles. Smilax scratching my calves, trumpet vine whipping my face, I ran til I gasped and finally reached the path. Cypresses and woodpeckers were one thing, and enormous gators were another. When Zara caught up, she was laughing. "He wouldn't hurt you," she told me.

"I'd rather not take my chances," I said.

Zara dropped against a fallen log. And held out her arms. "C'mere," she told me, and we stretched out on the pillowy moss.

"Thank you for sharing this with me," she said.

Our foreheads touched. We were gonna kiss again, really kiss for the first time in days, and a sweet need tugged between my legs. "Thank you for showing me all this."

Zara pulled me closer. Her thigh parted mine, and she kissed me. It was another of those delicious slow kisses, gentle, like she was trying to figure me out with her lips. I rested a palm on her cheek. I'd dreamed of this softness, soft skin and soft bodies, all curves melting into each other. "You feel so good," Zara said against my lips.

"You too," I whispered. The whole forest seemed to hold us, and we were alone with it. Our kiss rose into something wild and perfect, like a lightning storm or a driving rain. Zara's hand slid between us. She thumbed my nipple through my tank top, and I pressed against her thigh. She pushed it higher. When I cupped her breast, she gasped. Zara wasn't wearing a bra, and her nipples were button-hard.

"Here." She scooted back. "Take off your clothes. Please? I want to feel you against me."

A few days ago, I would've blushed. I would've made an excuse, something dumb, but life had shifted in ways I never imagined, and I shucked off everything. Zara lifted her dress. When she flipped on top of me, her warm pussy pressed mine. We kissed, and I couldn't think, 'cause her hips were rocking, and my clit slid against her. I thought girls rubbing against each other was a porn thing, like they did it for guys, but that sweet pressure made me bite my lip. I was getting wet, opening up, and Zara was slippery against me. When she lifted up a bit and quickly spread us both, I couldn't help but gasp. I swear I felt her clit, like a tiny, plump little nub.

I whimpered when she moved away, but her hand moved between my legs. When a slim finger slipped inside me, she pressed a place inside me guys could never find, and her thumb brushed my clit. Barely grazing me, she petted like I was delicate and special. No one had ever been so gentle. I couldn't help wiggling my hips.

I dared to slip a palm between her legs. Her pussy was silky-soft, and her lips were delicate, like flowers, those thin, frilled edges. When I slid a finger into her, she purred and spread her legs. I didn't quite know how to touch her, so I moved my thumb like she did, barely skimming her, like I'd stroke a newborn kitten. I snuggled closer. Zara stopped for a moment to shed her dress. Before she settled next to me again, I only grabbed a quick peek, but her nipples were tight and red. I must have pinched them hard. Her skin was such a pretty brown, and I didn't think they would be pink.

But her thumb slipped back to my clit, and I stopped thinking. We were curled close together, stretched on our backs. The swamp seemed to breathe with us. We were together in it, cradled in the forest's dark, secret heart. I smelled warm earth, wind in the trees, the sharp scent of water. Time stretched like a lazy cat. That perfect tension built, and Zara's thumb never sped up.

When her breath came quicker, I realized she was as close as me. I arched my hips up. Zara made a small, sweet sound, and her pussy tightened, tightened, tightened. She seemed to quiver there, motionless, then both of us broke like a wave in the same shattering moment. Maybe we gasped or pressed closer or bucked our hips. I was lost in it. I never thought it could be like that. I never believed it, or believed in it. Sex always felt like racing myself to a finish. But we were two people alone with the trees and earth and shimmering green, and we were beautiful.

Eventually, our hands moved. Still as forest creatures, we cuddled together on that moss. "I'm scared to talk, 'cause I don't want to ruin it," Zara whispered.

"Me too." She smelled warm, like herself, like everything I ever wanted.

Quiet, we stayed that way for a long time. She was warm, cushiony instead of hard-edged. I never wanted to leave. But we had to sit up eventually. We had to get up, and we had to join the world again. When Zara shifted back, I opened my eyes.

Her nipples were still red. I didn't think I pinched them that hard. I bit back a gasp when I realized they weren't nipples at all, but berries, red and bright, like holly or sumac. Hard, nubby little things, they stood stiff. I scrambled backward and hit rough cypress bark. Under my thumb, her clit had felt like that. And between her legs—those delicate lips—I leapt up and stared.

Zara squinched her eyes shut.

I stammered something, all nonsense. My heart kicked up.

"It's not what you think," Zara said, and her arms went around her chest. "Emerald, just listen for a second."

"You felt like flower petals," I managed.

"Please." Zara dropped her head, and her dark hair fell in her face, like she wanted to hide from me. I knew that feeling. It would've ached if I wasn't so scared. "I'm so lonely. You understand that. You could stay here with me, if you wanted to. We can be together here forever and always, Emerald."

"What are you?" That realization came slowly, then all at once. Zara couldn't do magic. She *was* magic. I thought fairy tales weren't real. I thought there was nothing past what I could touch, a long, blank, endless nothing. I didn't know which was scarier.

Zara seemed so small, no clothes on, hunched next to that fallen log. "I just want to be with you," she said. "We'll never be lonely. We can take care of each other and be in love and be happy. I want to wake up next to you in the morning, Emerald."

"No." I was hugging myself, too. We were naked in the forest, far apart.

"Emerald." Zara grabbed my arm, and I jerked away. "Please. I waited for you. You always went on walks, and I saw you, and I finally got up enough courage to talk to you—"

"You *watched me*?" I didn't know fear had a taste. But it does, like blood and pennies, sharp and bitter. I snatched my clothes and held them in front of me.

"Please don't go." Her eyes filled. "Please stay with me, at least for a little while if you don't want to stay for always—"

"No." I clutched my clothes to my chest.

"Please. You hate those people because they don't accept you." Zara drew her knees up to her chest. "I just want the—"

I held my clothes in front of me, and I ran. I leapt roots. Mud splashed up my legs and hid those pretty tattoos. She wasn't a person. She was something else entirely.

"Emerald!" Zara shouted, already far away.

I didn't look back.

BACK IN MY CAR, I floored it. It's strange how you think something as flimsy as a door can save you. It's hope more than belief. Maybe that hope's so strong it holds those bad things on the other side of the door, driving them back with nothing more than wishes. I could've believed it. I could've believed a lot of things then.

"What's wrong?" Jett called when I slammed inside and ducked in my room. Luckily, no one else was home. "Emmy? You okay?"

"Fine!" I shouted back. *I hooked up with something that isn't human.*

"You just seemed really, uh, freaked." He sounded far away, like the house had warped and stretched between us.

"No, I'm good!" I buried my head in my pillow. Halfway down the path, I'd stopped and pulled my clothes on. I wanted to strip them off and shower, like I could wash off all that fear. Zara wasn't human. I had no place to slot her or name to call her.

Tired from running and other things I didn't want to think about, I fell asleep. If you'd have asked, I'd have told you I was too scared to sleep, but I passed out anyway. Maybe I was so terrified that my body shut down rather than face whatever waited in that swamp.

When I woke up, the sun was setting in pinks and golds. Dirty laundry humped up in piles. At the bottom of my bed, an old patchwork quilt tangled with sheets, a blanket, my old teddy bear. Once I was a little girl. Once I'd believed in fairy tales but then I grew up and decided they were a dream. I walked in the swamp 'cause I thought nothing could touch me. I shoved up and stripped off my clothes. New ones felt a little bit better.

When I went in the kitchen, Mama didn't turn from the stove. In that harsh white light, all her grays showed, and she looked like an old woman, hunchback and tired. "Sit your ass down," she snapped. "You tell me where the hell you were all day."

She hadn't seen me leave. Had she seen me come home? Her question had no right answer. Mama was good at those. I wondered if it was her, or if all mothers had that talent.

"I told you to sit down, Emmy Ann," Mama said.

That name—that was a little girl's name. After what I saw in that swamp, I wasn't a little girl anymore. "Emerald." My voice didn't waver. "My name is Emerald."

"You think I don't know that when I gave it to you?" She gestured with her wooden spoon like she was holding a sword. "Sit your ass down. You and I need to have a conversation."

The day was bad enough. I wouldn't add a lecture from Mama on top of it. I'd seen a person who wasn't a person at all, and beside that, standing up to Mama felt like nothing. Why would she scare me? She was human. "No," I told her. "You're gonna yell at me for something. I'm twenty-one years old. You can talk like I'm an adult, but you aren't gonna sit me down and shout like I'm ten."

Mama studied me for a moment. "Sit down," she told me.

That anger coiled up again. It tangled in my chest and climbed my throat, and I thought for a moment I'd strangle. Everyone thought I'd shut up and do what I was told. "No," I said again. Mama was gonna lose it—when she was real mad, she'd shout something like, *You don't talk to your mother like that. You respect your elders, you hear me, Emmy Ann? I brought you into this world and I can take you out of it.*

"You were in that swamp again." Mama spoke it like a statement, not a question, and I knew I was in real trouble, more than I'd ever been before.

"So what if I was?" I wanted to plant my back against that sorry-ass kitchen wall. I would've felt those familiar nicks and scratches bump under my hand, and they'd have felt something like safe. But stepping back would look weak, and I was too mad for weak. I was grown. I had a job and my own choices and damn if she'd tell me different.

The evening light drew her in sharp, hard shadows. It showed her wrinkles. Mama looked like a storybook witch, like she'd lived long and lived hard, all gray roots and gnarled fingers. "You don't go in that swamp. I told you and told you and damn if you ever listen to me, Emmy Ann!"

"I told you, my name is Emerald," I said.

"Whatever the fuck you wanna call yourself!" Her spoon hit the counter like God's own judgment.

I looked at that spoon. I looked at her. A lifetime in the chicken plant had shriveled her up, like it sucked down her insides and left her hollowed-out. That made me almost as angry as her yelling. Life had beaten her down before she had a chance. "I went in that swamp 'cause I wanted to," I said. "I heard what you said. But I made my own choices."

"What the hell d'you even mean?" she snapped. "What the fuck d'you do out there, Emmy Ann?"

I couldn't hide anymore. She could like it or not like it, but I was tired of lying. I could've pretended I wasn't out there with Zara. For a moment, I thought about it. But lying would've meant denying who I was. I stood in that tiny kitchen next to the battered table where I'd done my homework, and my toes curled into the rag rug my gramma made. I'd lied there so many times. I was Emerald, and I was done with it.

"I went out there to meet a girl," I said. "I like girls. I mean, like I'm bisexual. You can like it or not, but that's who I am."

Diamond must've overheard us shouting and heaved herself off the couch. Her moon-face appeared in the doorway, and she was grinning. I wanted to smack that smile off her face. From the kitchen table, Jett and Aunt Tabby stared. The moment held and held, silent, tearing.

Mama finally spoke. "What are you saying, Emerald Ann Joiner?"

"I said I like girls." I spoke loudly, like I had nothing to be ashamed of. And there was nothing shameful about it. If there was shame, they handed it to me. I could refuse it. I would never wear anyone else's shame again—not for liking girls, not for my job, and not for being a Joiner, either.

"You like girls." Mama spoke in that same cool voice again, the dangerous one. "You know what people in this town will say about me if they find out you're running around with women?"

"My choices are mine." I balled my fists and I believed it. That anger burst into full flower. I was myself. "Who I am has nothing to do with you, and I won't change it 'cause you're afraid of what people will say."

Don't, my brother mouthed. *Stop it.*

They could accept me or not. Zara accepted me. Something in my chest slid sideways. Zara wasn't human. "I won't stop it," I said. "I am who I am and I'm not apologizing anymore."

"Then you can get your fancy self outta this house," Mama replied, and my aunt nodded along with her. "I'm sick and tired of your bullshit. I won't have you running around this town tattooed up like a whore and saying you're one of those lesbos. You're not that way. I raised you better than that."

She gripped the counter behind her like she was clinging to a ledge, ready to tumble over, and holding on was her last best hope. Below her shorts, her feet were bare. Those bare feet with pink-painted toes almost broke my heart. They seemed so vulnerable, the saddest part of her. But anger crumpled her face, and she meant every word.

Mama and Aunt Tabby, Diamond and Jett, they all watched me. We were five strangers in that little room, people crammed together by accidents of birth. That house was like a bus station. We moved in and out of it, never staying, always glancing warily at one another. It would be like that until someone agreed to change it. They wouldn't try, or they didn't know how, and one person couldn't do it alone.

"You want me to leave?" I asked. "Then I'll leave. You can kick me out like you kicked out Jackson. You don't love us anymore 'cause we're doing the best we can? Then you can fuck right off, Mama. I'm done with you." Back straight, I walked outta that kitchen like I was striding a catwalk.

"What the hell was that?" Aunt Tabby shouted behind me. "You respect your mama, y'hear me?"

I ignored her.

I could've flung myself on that bed and cried. I could've run back there and begged. The girl I loved wasn't a girl at all, and Mama had kicked me out of the house for nothing more than being myself. I might've lost it.

I grabbed a duffle bag and packed. Last of all, I grabbed my cash, hidden in an old backpack under my bed—every week, I stopped at the bank, and I deposited all the money Mama didn't take, and Jett and I didn't need—usually only fifty bucks or so, and that ran out quick. Glaring, the tellers touched my money like it would make them sick. They knew where it came from. But I was done caring about that.

I wasn't scheduled to work that night. I didn't much care. I had nowhere else to go.

"Hey, Luna!" Noah called as I walked into the club's weird twilight. "I didn't think you were on tonight!"

"I'm not." I leaned against the bar. "I thought I'd come in anyway. Not much to do at home." Not like I had a home, or a girlfriend—if I'd ever had a girlfriend. While we curled in that swamp and kissed each other, I thought I did. That hurt more than Mama. Fear was eroding into sadness. I couldn't love someone who wasn't human. *She's not a someone,* I told myself. *She's something else entirely.*

"Well, head on back." Noah grabbed a Coke and slid it down the bar. "Anyone bothers you, lemme know."

Back in the dressing room, I didn't tell Alyssa why Mama kicked me out, but she said I could stay with her for a little while. I was glad about that. Least I knew where I'd lay my head. "Imma head home 'bout midnight," she told me. "Lucky's daddy says he has to work in the morning, and he can't stay longer than that." She swooped me into a hug. Alyssa smelled like roses, and I wished for Zara's honeysuckle. "I'm so sorry, Emmy," she told me.

"Thanks," I said, and it should've made me feel better. Alyssa and I had been besties since we were five. It didn't matter. She didn't know anything about me.

I slipped into Luna. When you need money, you do what you have to, even if life is crumbling to pieces. The guys distracted me. They wrapped their arms around my waist and breathed into my ear. I tried not to wish they were Zara. Rubbing on those guys, I stepped through dance after dance, but I gave myself one heartsick indulgence. "Hey," I said to the DJ, "do Nine Inch Nails's 'Sunspot' for me next, will you?"

"Cool," he replied, half-zoned, already high on something. Maybe you'd have to be.

I stalked onstage in those fat platform heels. I wore black and chains and a leather collar; men watched me from the dark beyond the stage lights. The song was slow, and I worked it, shook my ass, climbed that pole, dropped my top and grabbed my tits. I mouthed words, and music thrummed through me. I was part of that throbbing beat, everything I wanted and could never have. Eyes begging me to stay, Zara had been so sad. She wasn't a person, but maybe I'd run too soon. Maybe I should've listened, even if I was scared. The music filled me up, and I held it against the day's raw misery. All those men, those people watching, they made me into Emmy Joiner, just like my mother had. I would never be anything else for them. I tried not to look in their eyes but they stared. I was naked, and they thought they knew me.

My vines were beautiful under the lights, dark, marking me as something wild and unknowable and strange. They were mine. Zara had put them there, but I wanted them. *Who are you, Emerald Joiner?* someone might've asked, and I'd have pointed to those tattoos. *I'm that,* I'd have told them. *That's me, right there, take it or leave it.* I could've broken down. I let the music take me instead.

When I stepped off that stage, I found three twenties tucked in my thong. It was money. It meant nothing. They wanted something, but it wasn't me.

"That was amazing, Luna," Noah said when I hit the bar.

"Thanks." I swiped at my face and drained my Coke. I wouldn't think about Mama. I wouldn't think about Zara.

"Car still running okay?" he asked.

"Sure," I said.

"Lemme know if you ever need anything," he told me. "I'm always here to help you out, you know that, right?"

"Hey, girl." Alyssa touched my shoulder. She was wearing street clothes. "I'm headed home, okay? Key's under the doormat."

"Thanks." I got up and hugged her. One more time, I wished for Zara. No one at that club knew me. They might've called me Luna, but I was Emmy Ann there, one more poor girl scrambling to catch whatever leftovers other people tossed away. Alyssa opened the door to a dark night, a glimpse of stars, then shut it behind her. Girls sat on laps. Hazy in the cigarette smoke, they seemed soft-edged, blurred, like men could mold them into daydreams. I was one of them. When I picked up my Coke, Noah was studying me.

"You and Alyssa partying after work?" He smiled a little. "Do I get an invite?"

Noah knew I lived with Mama and Aunt Tabby, but it was the kind of thing you overlooked, like someone's bad breath or underarm sweat. And he'd find out I left—the club ran on rumor and gossip and catty backbiting. "My mom kicked me out," I said. "I'm staying with Alyssa for a while."

He set down his rag and rested his elbows on the bar. "So your mama made you leave?"

I hadn't thought about blurring the truth, and I cussed myself. I could've said I moved out. "Yeah, she did," I said. "She finally lost it about my dancing, I guess."

"Really?" he asked. "You've been dancing for six months."

I could tell him or not tell him. No one knew me, and maybe it was time they did. I was tired of being Emmy Joiner, and Luna, all those masks I kept between me and the outside world. It was time to take them off. "Yeah," I said. "But she found out I like girls, and that put her over the edge."

I didn't blush. I didn't stutter, or look down, or hide behind my hair. Instead, I watched Noah's face cloud into something like confusion. "You like girls?" he asked. "What d'you mean?"

I drained my Coke. "I mean I'm bi, and I'd rather be with girls." The music seemed far away, and my words were too real for that Christmas light glow.

"You're like that?" Noah's expression changed, but I couldn't read it, good or bad.

"Yeah," I said, 'cause I couldn't back down then.

"Huh." It could've meant anything. Dread brooded in my belly.

"Imma go dance," I said. "I'll let you know when I need walked out." I left him there at the bar. Maybe I shouldn't have told him, but I was tired of it. I'd left Zara and Mama. I'd lost all my choices, and the world cleared into bare bones. That happens when you have nothing else to lose. You go all-in 'cause there's nothing else left.

I smoked and drank and laughed. I worked tables of guys. Maybe they liked me not caring what they thought. It made me untouchable somehow. "You wanna go out back?" one asked, arm tightening around me.

"Not really, no," I told him instead of giggling.

He blushed, and then bought three dances. "Your tats are amazing," he said when it was over.

"Thanks," I replied, straightening up.

"I wish…" His eyes were sad, like Zara's, and he stopped. Once I would have giggled, or maybe asked what he wished for, but I walked away instead.

Noah passed me drinks when I hit the bar, but he didn't say much. He was distant and I finally saw it: That distance said something about him, not me. When Mama flew off the handle, it wasn't my fault. She was fed-up with an idea she'd created, and I had very little to do with it.

The club seemed so small then. It was all a set-up. Men came in, and we gave them a night of fairy tales. It didn't last. They would go back to their gritty, sweaty jobs, their worried nights, the women they didn't like who didn't like them. Usually I thought about handing them dreams, and it made me sort of happy. I could give them something, and it might make life a little better, a little more bearable. But it didn't matter, not in the end. It would never get better for those men. They'd slave away til they died or got too hurt to work anymore. Old men, bitter, I imagined them sitting on porches, counting time-rotted dreams. They'd hope in Jesus and the lottery. Neither would come through. I saw their whole lives, from their unwanted beginnings to their lonely, sputtering deaths, and I could've run outta that club crying. They were drowning men, clutching life's soaked remnants. They'd sink in the end.

Men gathered their cigarettes and paid their bar tabs and drove into the night. I changed into shorts and a tank top. When I appeared at the bar, the house lights were up. The sticky floor shone; empty glasses and balled-up cocktail napkins scattered the tables. Its party had moved on; real life had swooped in and blown away the dream. "You mind walking me out?" I asked Noah.

"No." He stopped counting bottles and came around the bar. "I wanted to talk to you anyway. C'mon."

I should've smiled. There was nothing that should've worried me, but I worried anyway. Something wasn't right. I held my bag tight as we passed through the door and into the parking lot. Noah stopped as we rounded the corner. The lot was dark, but the trees beyond were darker. Night seemed to snag and linger in them. Normally, it might've scared me, but that darkness felt like an old friend.

"Listen, Luna." Noah ruffled his hair. "I'm worried about you."

I'd had enough of people worried about me. I might've relaxed, but he'd offered something, and I knew what he was thinking. "I'm fine," I told him. "Really. I'm staying at Alyssa's, and I'll save enough for my own place in a few—"

Noah stepped closer. He tucked a strand of hair behind my ear, and I went as still as a hunted creature in that humming swamp. "You can stay with me."

"Thank you," I said carefully. "But I'm good at Alyssa's. It's really kind of you to—"

"Emmy." Noah was watching me, not that night-forest. "Your car's half-dead and you don't have anywhere to go. You can stay with me, honey." He was too close, his breath in my face. It smelled like cherry Lifesavers. Strange, the things you grab when you're panicking, those sensations that hit hard and won't leave. "You don't need to stay with Alyssa."

His eyes reminded me of the men watching beside the stage, the greedy ones that saw something and wanted it. Cicadas thrummed, and something rustled in those leaning trees. On most nights, those sounds would have sent me shivering. Instead, they seemed to feed some deep-down bravery.

"I'm good with Alyssa," I told him. My voice stayed cautious. The humidity clung to my back, and it seemed too hot for darkness.

Noah's shoulders sagged. Hunched into himself, a bird in the rain, he drew back. "You and Alyssa have a thing, don't you?"

"No," I said. "Why would you think that? She has Lucky, and—"

"I've been trying." His voice was small against the swamp sounds, so dim it almost drowned in cicada-hum. "Y'know, I've tried so hard, Emmy. I did everything but tell you straight out. I never asked for anything—I know how those guys inside are. I don't wanna be like them."

"You're not," I assured him, reflexively, like it was my job to make him feel better. "There's nothing with Alyssa and me—we've been friends since kindergarten. But—Noah—" I drew a shuddery breath. "You're my boss." Mama would've told me, *Don't shit where you eat,* and that was an ugly way to say it, but she was right. Girls like me had to be careful. A man with power over us would only snatch more.

"Is that all?" Noah straightened. Uncurling, he took my hands in his. I managed not to flinch back. "Emmy, that doesn't matter. I'd be so good to you. If it's the thing with girls—listen, you think you like girls, but you're confused. You need someone to keep you safe, keep you away from all this. You shouldn't be in that club."

Gently, I pulled back. Untamed, quietly savage, the swamp loomed around us, like it might creep closer and swallow us both. Normally, I would've shivered. But it felt as familiar as a soft blanket. "It's not just that," I said carefully. "I like you. I do. And if things were different—" I struggled. He was kind, and I hated hurting him. "I don't like many guys, Noah. Not at all."

He pressed his lips together and glanced at the swamp, then shivered. "Did someone scare you, Emmy? That happens to girls sometimes, scares them away from men. It's not like that. I can show you."

I ached. Noah was like everyone in that town, small-minded, stuffing me into slots I'd never fit. "No one hurt me," I said, and those trees, their leaning branches, the dripping moss and wilding brush, they lent me a strength I'd never had. Green and growing, it roiled like a brushfire in my chest. "This is me—this is who I am. I'm sorry."

Drawing his elbows close, Noah kicked at the dirt. "Of fucking course. I end up liking the girl who wants another girl. Something like this always happens, y'know? I do my goddamn best. I try so hard not to be like those other guys. Maybe I should be. That's what girls want, isn't it?"

"It's not what I want," I told him.

"Of-fucking-course-not, 'cause you think you want pussy instead. You don't. You'll figure it out." His expression twisted into meanness. "You'll figure it out, Emmy, and I'll be gone. Don't ask me again. I'm done with you." Jaw clenched, Noah kicked another dusky-dry puff of dust. Gravel grated as he stomped back to the club. I could've collapsed. Goddamn him. Goddamn all those men who thought women owed them something. I hefted my bag and strode to my car. With my luck, it wouldn't start. I'd have to ask him for help, and he'd leave me there—

A hand closed over my wrist, and I bit back a scream. Noah wasn't done. But when I whirled, Isaac Wheeler leered at me. Fear clotted my throat, sharp and bitter-black.

"I been waiting for you, Emmy Joiner," he said.

"I told you no." Cicada-shrieks soared to a deafening thrum. That swamp was meaner, closer. You could lose yourself in it—lose yourself and never come back. It should've scared me.

"And I offered you good money." Isaac's breath reeked of stale beer and cigarettes. "I offered you three hundred and fifty, girl. You think you're too good for me? I know you fuck around. The whole town knows it."

"I don't." When I tried to back away, his grip tightened. He knew what he was gonna do. Isaac had already made a decision; he'd come to that dark parking lot and waited.

"This can go easy or it can go real bad." He yanked me closer. I cringed back. Isaac was already hard, and maybe that frightened me worst: He got off on scaring me. When he grabbed my hair and forced my head back, I knew I was fucked. Isaac pushed his tongue in my mouth, and I almost gagged from the rotten taste. I wouldn't open my teeth, and his thin tongue licked my lips.

"What the *fuck*?" someone shouted, and Isaac jerked back.

"Just some fun," he snapped. "What's—"

A fist flashed, and I flew back as his nose crunched with a shuddering, audible crack.

"I told you I'd beat your ass if you touched her!" Noah shouted. Isaac was down, and Noah kicked his gut, his crotch. Isaac screamed as his fingers broke under Noah's boot. When Noah booted his stomach, a soft squeak slipped from him. You'd think a beat-down like that would be loud, but it wasn't. Noah's foot thumped on flesh; Isaac let out little whimpers. Soon he was curled up and crying, and Noah spit in his face.

"Get the fuck outta here," he said. "If I ever see you again, I'll kill you."

Isaac scrambled up and ran.

"Hey, Emmy." Noah swooped me into his arms. I'd frozen, watching him, unable to look away. "Hey," he said, rocking me back and forth. "You're safe. You're safe now. I was so worried something like this would happen to you. I told you, this is no place for a girl like you."

I was too scared to cry. Noah smelled like Old Spice and cherry Lifesavers. "You're okay, you're safe," he murmured over and over. Relieved, I melted into him. My heart beat like a panicked bird, fluttering, trying to escape. I took deep breaths. It was almost working until I realized Noah's lips were against my neck.

"You taste good," he whispered.

"This isn't—" I started.

"Shhh." He kissed my neck, then moved up to my ear. "Shh, Emmy," he said over the swamp's night-songs. "Shh, honey. This is how it's supposed to be. See how good this is?"

"Let go," I told him, and when I struggled, he hugged me tighter. That fear rose again, sharp-tasting and bright. "Stop it."

"This can be so nice," Noah said, and his dick pressed my stomach. He arched his hips into me, and nausea rolled somewhere in my midsection. "See how nice this is?" His mouth came down on mine.

No one was gonna touch me again. No one was gonna tell me who I was and what I wanted. I wrenched back and broke loose. Almost amazed at my own strength, I paused for one slivered moment. Noah snatched at me. My hands went around his neck, and I squeezed tight.

I shouldn't have been able to do it. I knew that as I felt his pulse flutter under my fingers. But all that anger bubbled up—anger at Mama, anger at him, anger at that town determined to make me feel small. Everyone tried to tell me who I was and who I needed to be. I wouldn't let it happen anymore.

Eyes bulging, Noah dropped to his knees. Parking lot dust grated and puffed up, a dry smell, like hungry earth. The swamp hummed louder, meaner, as angry as me. My hands squeezed tight as trumpet vine. What was I doing? I shouldn't do this. But something was roiling in me, green, vicious, wicked and gleaming. My thumbs pressed deeper.

In that sweet, swallowing darkness, my arms were changing. Vines began at my fingertips and climbed upward, black, coiling, and a terrible strength infused me. Noah would never hurt anyone. He'd never hurt anyone else again. *Yes,* that swamp-chorus exalted. *Make him hurt. Make him pay for it.* Every cicada-hum stiffened my grip. Those shrieking tree frogs joined me, those birds, the towering trees and clinging vines. I felt the white alligator then. I felt the ivory-bills, and the small, creeping creatures, and the moon brooding on wind-rustled leaves. Black vines writhed up my arms, fingers to shoulder, down my chest and over my stomach. They met the tattoos on my legs and snaked downward. I was Emerald. Standing with my feet spread apart, all that strength bent into my hands, I knew what I was doing. Green overtook me, bloomed in me. As Noah's arms flailed, his hands clawed at mine. I squeezed harder. In the movies, death comes fast, but this wasn't fast at all. Noah's tongue stuck out, and his eyes rolled. He scrambled to stand but I held him down.

"You're not gonna tell me who I am," I told him.

He tried to speak but no words came out. His feet scrabbled at the dirt.

"I see who you are," I said. "You pretend to like me, but you just want something. You're exactly like the rest of them. You think you can tell me who to be?" My thumbs dug into him. "This is who I am, you bastard."

Noah's arms were going limp, and his hands had no strength left. He was gonna fall but if I let go I wouldn't finish it. His hand slapped my leg, my arms, those vines, dark on my pale skin. I was Emerald Joiner, and no one would ever hurt me again. Noah's good looks went ravaged and old. I saw him. He was like all the others, and I was finished with them.

Noah's eyes rolled back. When they closed, he flopped into my hands. My thumbs hurt, and I let go. Noah crumpled like a doll. He was gone, and something broke in me then. That green feeling shattered, and I was one person alone in a parking lot. I understood then why murderers stare at their hands. You can't believe you could do that. You look at a corpse and you look at your hands and you think, *There was a person and now there's not anymore. My hands did that.*

You'd think you'd panic. I didn't. I stood over that body and I made myself look at it. Noah was smaller dead than he'd looked alive, a little heap of a thing. The police would uncurl him. They'd say, *Who did this? Whose fingerprints are on his neck?* Then they'd find me.

And even if they didn't find me, or they did and I got out of it, I'd never escape, not really, not Noah or anyone else in that town. I'd always be Emmy Joiner, a broke-ass whore, nothing and no one to anybody. They didn't know me. They didn't want to. *Get out*, I imagined Alyssa saying. *I wouldn't have someone that perverted around Lucky. You always looked at me when we changed, didn't you?*

I could tell them who I was. They wouldn't care. They'd do their best to cram me into the box they made, and if I refused to fit, they'd force me. I stood in that dark parking lot and I knew it. Then I reached for the swamp and it was there, throbbing with life, with a glory I'd never imagined. Dazed, I stumbled to my car. Zara would understand. She'd say, *You did the right thing. You didn't let him hurt you, and you stood up for who you are.*

In that close, panting dark, I felt vines twining my body. When I glanced down, the dark marks on my arms were still there. They were mine. I was with the swamp, and the swamp was with me.

Mama had shoved me in a box, like I wasn't a person at all. Like Zara. I'd treated Zara the same way. She'd never hurt me, and she could have. She could've kept me in that swamp forever and ever, even if I said no. My tattoos told me that. *You're not human*, I told her, like Mama said, *You're not that way*, or Noah told me, *You're not like that.* I tried to show them who I was, and they said, *No, you can't be that way. We'll change you if we have to.* Nothing could break the confines of their small lives. This town was full of jailers, and they kept themselves locked up.

Zara asked for understanding. She showed me who she was, and I said, *You're not human*. Was it any different, really? More misery settled down. No one needed to tell me the answer.

I could've ignored it. When it suits us, we ignore a lot of things. Brave people have the courage to look. I lived in a town full of cowards, but I didn't have to be one. If nothing else taught me that, my hands on Noah's neck had.

You hold on tight, Emmy Ann, Talitha told me. Around me, the swamp sang a hundred soaring songs. That strange power flowed through me again, different from me but not different at all. It was me. I had it all along. Zara had told me that. *You could do it if you believed you could.*

My car started, and I drove home, back to Mama's house. I knew what I had to do and where I had to go. That town would try to hold me, but I wouldn't let it. Those people would pin me down like one of those old-timey butterflies in a glass case. They would say, *This is Emmy Ann Joiner. This is who she is, and she will never escape it. You can't change who you are.*

I couldn't escape it, not there. I drove down that long, straight swamp highway, and wind played in my hair. Wet heat sucked at me; I might've hated it, but it felt like home. I thought of Mama's hands, their swollen joints and arthritic knuckles. She'd done the best she could. Everyone in this town did the best they could, and it was never enough. Life would break you. It would squeeze you dry and wring you out and leave you with nothing but your own empty hands. People like us Joiners, we'd never grab a toehold. The deck was stacked and the dice were loaded. We spent our days falling through empty air, nothing to catch us, no bottom to hit. It never changed. It never would.

I'll get my own place, I said. *I'll get an education.* I could've laughed as I threaded down those narrow roads, small cuts through deep swampland. Even if I managed to escape the body in that lonely parking lot, life would stay snatched-breath desperate, at my mama's house or my own, educated or not. Gravel grated as I pulled into the driveway, too loud over screaming cicadas and screechy tree frogs. I was done with the loneliness, the defeat, the you're-not-good-enough. I was Emerald, and I was finished.

I parked. My mother and brother, sister and aunt slept, wrapped in their own secret dreams. I'd never know them. They were their own people, misunderstood, maybe trying to do their best but busy holding one another down. Crabs in a bucket, Mama always said. I didn't know she was talking about herself.

High above, stars hung like promises; the moon was high and fat and round as an orange. When I stepped into the yard, tall grass brushed my calves. That warm swamp-smell hit my nose, standing water and deep mud, safe as it had always been. I walked around the trailer. There was my old window, and from the yard, I heard Diamond's familiar snoring. I wished I could talk to her. *We're sisters*, I'd have said. *We had differences but they don't matter, not really. I love you. I know you love me, deep down, behind all that sadness. You're trapped, and you want someone to blame.* She'd laugh, maybe cry, and stomp away. *You like girls, Emmy Ann,* she'd say. *That's gross, and I don't want my baby around it.* That baby would grow up like her, small-minded in a small town. I ached for it. I hope she woke up and got out one day.

Cicada hum swelled like the symphonies I'd never heard. At the end of the path, I kicked off my sandals. I wouldn't need them anymore. I wouldn't need so many things. I'd walked past my mother's house and come home. When I passed under those sheltering cypresses, night scooped me into its arms. I would never be alone again.

"Emerald?" a soft voice called.

"I'm sorry," I told Zara. I didn't see her, but I felt her, a soft breeze on my cheek. "I shouldn't've run. I should've listened. You won't hurt me. And you deserve—" I struggled. "They try to put me in a box. I did the same to you."

A familiar hand slipped into mine. Cypresses hid the sky, and the dark was thick as a blanket, too thick for me to see. "You came back," Zara said. Her breath tickled my ear, humidity rising from a hundred little pools. "Will you stay for a little bit?"

"I'll stay as long as you want me," I told her. "There's nothing out there but meanness." I reached for her, but touched nothing. "It helped me." I whispered it like a confession, one of those things Catholics save for priests in stark black boxes. Zara would know what "it" meant. "I needed it, and it came."

"You understand now." A hand brushed my hair aside. I tilted my head to it, but it had gone, or it was never there. "It'll always be there for you, Emerald. I've been waiting."

Inside me, beauty burst to full flower. I was vivid, growing, strong as those vines. I didn't reach for Zara. I knew her. She was in the alligator, the ivory-bills, the streams and the trees and the dark-tannin water. The wind whispered hymns to her. Water babbled with love. As I melted into her, the strength of trees lifted me. Oh, she was lovely, dark, full of secrets. The ferocity of her night-black panther rooted around my heart. I was complete, free. I had become everything I dreamed.

"It'll always be awful out there," Zara told me, and her voice was a brush-rustle of loveliness. "They don't want anything different. C'mon, Emerald."

We were safe. I felt her, all of her, the long stretch of rich, green forest breathing with me. Swamp was an ugly word, short and fat, but Zara was bright in the darkness. We were together in that vine-tangled beauty, and her lips were soft as new-green grass. I knew hawks and otters then, deer and boars and that sleek panther, a whole wild world untouched and unimaginable.

I stepped inside.

ACKNOWLEDGEMENTS

This book could never have happened without the help of many, many others. Thank you to my horror writing friends, especially my workshop group; you've given me so much kindness and so many opportunities. I'm regularly humbled by your graciousness and talent. Thanks for giving me a seat at the table, y'all.

If *Ink Vine* is my baby, Rebecca Cuthbert is the midwife. She was there for every step of the (startlingly short) labor—coaching, encouraging. *Ink Vine* is lovely because she helped make it that way. A long career in journalism taught me that editors are unsung heroes; they never get enough credit for making writers look good. My name may be on the cover, but Rebecca helped make it the book it became. Thank you, wonderfulest of editors. You're amazing.

It takes a special person to marry a writer. It's a certain kind of love, more patient and tolerant than most. Chris knows I will degenerate into crabbiness between projects; he weathers elation and despair, Chromebook after Chromebook. He fixes my plot holes—oh, the joy of marrying a literary critic!—and perhaps ginned up a good deal of Ink Vine, but we've both forgotten by now. Love, there aren't words for your amazingness, only thank yous. The book isn't dedicated to you because everything is dedicated to you anyway.

Elizabeth Broadbent left the South Carolina swamps for the Commonwealth of Virginia, where she lives with her three sons and husband. She's the author of *Naked & Famous* (ELJ Editions, 2023), *Ink Vine* (Undertaker Books), and *Blood Cypress*, coming out in 2025 with Raw Dog Screaming Press. Her speculative fiction has appeared with *Hyphen Punk*, *Tales to Terrify*, *If There's Anyone Left*, *Peunumbric*, and *The Cafe Irreal*, among others. During her long career as a journalist, her non-fiction appeared in places such as *The Washington Post*, *Insider*, and *ADDitude Magazine*.

www.writerelizabethbroadbent.com

ALSO BY ELIZABETH BROADBENT

Naked & Famous

Wrapped in a Burning Flag

Blood Cypress (Coming Soon)